KONG
THE 8TH WONDER OF THE WORLD™

THE NOVEL

SIMON AND SCHUSTER
First published in Great Britain in 2005 by Simon & Schuster UK LTD
Africa House, 64-78 Kingsway, London WC2B 6AH
A Viacom Company

Originally published in the USA by Harper Kids Entertainment,
an imprint of Harper Collins Children's Division, New York, 2005.

ISBN 1-416-91719-5

10 9 8 7 6 5 4 3 2 1

Printed by Cox and Wyman, Reading, Berkshire

www.simonsays.co.uk
www.kingkongmovie.com

KONG
THE 8TH WONDER OF THE WORLD™

THE NOVEL

Adapted by Laura J. Burns and Melinda Metz
Based on a Motion Picture Screenplay
by Fran Walsh & Philippa Boyens & Peter Jackson
Based on a Story by Merian C. Cooper and Edgar Wallace

SIMON AND SCHUSTER

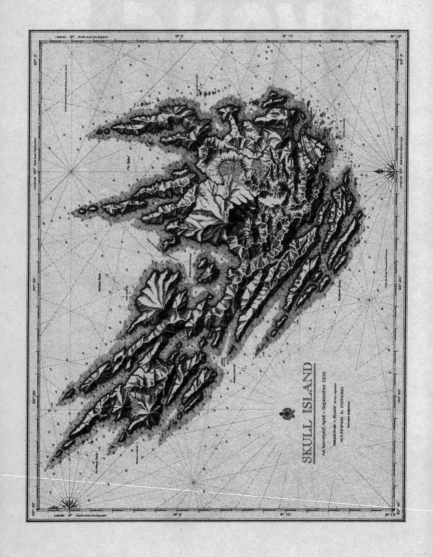

SKULL ISLAND

As Surveyed April – September 1936

1

"Engelhorn! Hoist up the mainsail! Raise the anchor!" Carl called to the captain of *The Venture*. Carl glanced behind him. The men who had invested in his movie weren't in sight—yet. Neither were the police. There was still time to escape with the canisters of film he'd already shot. The investors claimed he'd stolen them. But they were *his*. The movie was *his*. *He* was the director.

Carl was absolutely sure when he finished the movie it was going to make history *and* a huge pile of dough. He'd be able to pay back everybody he owed money to, including the investors and the captain, because Carl had found a film location that was nothing short of spectacular—Skull Island. No one knew the island was *The Venture's* actual destination yet, not even Captain Engelhorn or Hayes, Engelhorn's second in command. They would think Carl was crazy if he told them the truth. He wasn't sure even Mike and Herb, the men who had been on the crew of every movie he had made, would have agreed to come with him if he had told them where he planned on going.

But the island was the only place Carl's movie could be finished. He'd felt it in his bones the second he heard that Norwegian skipper talking about it. The skipper had rescued a castaway, barely alive. Before he'd died, the castaway had told the story of Skull Island. He'd said the place was shrouded in fog, cut off from the rest of the world. He claimed that it held the remains of an ancient civilization and that the people who lived there knew nothing of the modern age.

Carl was going to be the man to bring this discovery to the world with his movie. The castaway had given the skipper a map to the island—and Carl had bought it from the skipper almost before he finished telling the tale.

The moment Carl returned to New York with the footage shot on Skull Island, everyone would know his name. Every investor in town would want to back his next movie. Every actor in the country would want to star in a Carl Denham film. Carl took another look over his shoulder. The coast was still clear.

"Cast off!" he shouted. "We've got to leave." He guided

Ann Darrow, his new star, up the gangplank, hoping she wouldn't notice how nervous he was. The last thing he needed was for anyone on the boat to know he was worried about being arrested before the ship left the harbor.

Ann stared at the sailors rushing around *The Venture,* getting the ship ready, loading crates. Smoke was pouring from the stacks. Ann felt as if she was in a movie already. She could hardly believe any of this was real. Yesterday, she'd actually stolen an apple from a vendor's cart to keep from starving. Today, she was setting sail to make a movie starring Bruce Baxter and written by Jack Driscoll, her absolute favorite playwright.

Carl stepped over to Captain Engelhorn. They had a whispered conversation, and then Carl turned to Ann. "Can't you see we're in the presence of a VIP guest?" he said loudly. Ann felt her face flush. She'd never been called a VIP before. She was a lot more used to people throwing squishy tomatoes and slimy lettuce at her after she performed her slapstick comedy act. Some people laughed, and that was wonderful. But she got hit with moldy salad makings just as often.

"So you are ready for this voyage, Miss Darrow? You are not at all nervous?" the captain asked Ann. He had an accent. German, she thought.

"Nervous. No. Why? Should I be?" Ann asked, a few butterflies taking flight in her stomach.

Carl wished the captain would go do something—anything—on the ship. Something captainly. Something that didn't involve bothering Carl about when he would get paid —or worrying Carl's actress.

"I imagine you'd be terrified. It isn't every woman who would take such a risk," the captain answered. Ann's butterflies grew into buzzing bumblebees, pricking the walls of her stomach. If the captain thought she should be terrified, then—

Carl beamed when his assistant, Preston, rushed over and asked, "Why don't I show Miss Darrow to her cabin?" He whisked Ann away from the captain and his questions. Carl waited a moment, and then made his way through the ship's narrow corridors, heading toward his cabin. His star was safely taken care of. Now Carl needed to check in on his writer.

He opened his cabin door and ducked inside. Jack Driscoll sat at the table across from him. "If anyone comes to the door, don't open it," Carl told his friend. "You haven't seen me. Say I stuck my head down a toilet!" There was still a chance that the police might nab him.

Jack raised a dark eyebrow. Clearly something was up with his old friend Carl. But he didn't have the time to figure out what. "I can't stay. I have a rehearsal for which I am now"—he checked his watch—"three hours late." He threw a few pages across the table.

Carl frowned. "What's this?"

"The script," Jack answered.

Carl sat down. "Jack, there are only fifteen pages here."

"I know, but they're good! You've got fifteen good pages there, Carl!" Jack didn't have time for this. He had to get back to his play. It was almost opening night.

"Jack, you can't do this to me," Carl moaned. "I have a beginning, but I need a middle and an end! I gotta have something to shoot."

The ship's engines roared to life. Jack stood up. Through the portal, Carl saw a couple of sailors releasing ropes. He realized all he had to do was keep Jack on the ship for just a few more minutes. Then his problems would be solved.

"All right, fine. We might as well settle up," Carl said. He pulled out his checkbook.

Jack smiled. He'd been expecting begging and pleading

from Carl, maybe even a temper tantrum. "I've never known you to volunteer cash before."

"How does two grand sound?" Carl asked.

"Sounds great," Jack said as Carl wrote out the check and signed it with a flourish. "Voilà!" He gave the check to Jack.

"You wrote the words 'two grand,'" Jack said, his smile fading. The bank wouldn't cash that. Banks didn't use slang. Or have a sense of humor. He could feel the ship vibrating under his feet. The engine was going full steam. He had to get off *The Venture*—and fast.

"What's today's date? The twenty-ninth?" Carl asked.

"Come on, it's the twenty-fifth," Jack snapped.

Carl crumpled the new check. "Let me just . . . it'll only take a second."

Jack understood now. Carl didn't intend to pay him. He was trying to trap Jack onboard the ship! "Never mind, pay me when you get back!" he blurted out as he bolted from the cabin.

Carl leaned back in his chair and grinned. *Too late, Jackie,* he thought. *You'll have plenty of time to write that script now. It'll take us a few months to reach Skull Island.*

It was too late for the police and investors to grab

him, too. Now he could concentrate on making his masterpiece. He couldn't wait to get his first glimpse of Skull Island. The castaway had said it was sinking. Soon it would be lost forever.

But not before the great director Carl Denham captured the island—and every creature that lived there—on film!

Ann studied her small pile of clothing the next morning, wondering what she was going to wear to breakfast. All her clothes were ragged—it had been far too long since she'd had any money for new ones. She glanced into the closet of her cabin. It was filled with beautiful dresses and nightgowns. They were costumes for the movie. Would anyone notice if she borrowed one?

She chose a floral dress and slipped it on. She wanted to be able to hold her head high when she met Jack Driscoll. She'd seen all his plays. Half of all his plays, she corrected herself. She couldn't afford theater tickets, but it was easy to slip in with the rest of the crowd returning to their seats after intermission. Ann had gone to see the second half of a Jack Driscoll play whenever she wasn't performing herself—if you could call doing fake falls and taking pies to the face performing!

She took a deep breath, checked her hair in the mirror, and stepped out of her tiny cabin. It was easy enough to find the mess hall, although she couldn't be quite sure that the smell wafting through the ship really came from food.

When she stepped inside, Carl immediately jumped up from his seat. "Ann, come on over!" he cried. "Let me introduce you to the crew. This is Herb, our cameraman."

Preston pulled out a chair for Ann at the table while she shook Herb's hand.

"Delighted to meet you, ma'am," Herb said with a smile. "And may I say . . . what a lovely dress!"

Ann felt a blush creep up her cheeks. "Oh, this old thing?" she joked. "I just threw it on!"

"Isn't that one of the movie costumes?" Preston murmured to Carl.

Ann felt the tips of her ears get hot.

"What does a girl have to do to get breakfast around here?" she said quickly, trying to change the subject.

Carl grinned and turned to a crusty-looking man who was busy shaving a sailor with a straight razor and stirring a pot of porridge at the same time. "Lumpy!" Carl told him. "You heard the lady!"

Carl gestured to a young, handsome man sitting across

the table. He was scribbling in a notebook, ignoring everything going on around him. Ann's heart skipped a beat. She knew she had to be looking at Jack Driscoll.

"Ann," Carl said. "I don't believe you've met—"

"It's all right. I know who this is," Ann interrupted.

"How do you like your eggs?" Lumpy called to her.

"Scrambled," she told him. She nodded toward the man he was shaving. "No stubble," she added with a smile. Lumpy chuckled and gave her a half salute.

Ann turned back to Jack. "Thrilled to meet you," she told him. "It's an honor to be part of this."

"Gee, thanks," he said.

"Actually, I'm familiar with your work," Ann added.

"Really?"

She nodded. "The thing that I most admire is the way you have captured the voice of the common people."

"Well . . . that's my job," he said slowly.

"I'm sure you've heard this before, Mr. Driscoll," Ann said, leaning toward him. "If you don't mind me saying, you don't look anything like your photograph."

His eyes widened. "Excuse me?"

"Wait a minute!" Carl said. "Ann—"

"Well, he's so much younger in person," Ann said to

Carl. She turned back to Jack. "And much better looking."

"Ann!" Carl said. "Stop! Right there!" He wished he could slap his hand over her mouth, but she was too far away.

Ann stared at Jack. He stared back at her, frowning. She thought he should be smiling. She'd just given him a compliment she was sure any writer would love to hear. "I was afraid you might be one of those self-obsessed literary types," she rushed on. "You know, the tweedy twerp with his head in a book and a pencil up his—"

Someone behind Ann gave a loud cough. She glanced over her shoulder—and saw Jack Driscoll. The *real* Jack Driscoll. The one who exactly matched his picture in the theater programs she'd seen. Older than the man across from her. Tweedier. And obviously insulted.

Ann opened her mouth . . . but what could she say? She'd just made a fool of herself in front of one of the most talented writers in New York.

"You must be . . . Ann Darrow," the real Jack said. He couldn't believe she thought he looked old. Or that she thought Mike the soundman was better looking than he was! Or that she didn't like his favorite suit!

Ann had to get out of there. She jumped up from the table and ran out onto the deck. Preston followed.

"Help me, Preston," she moaned. "How do I get off this boat?"

"It didn't go *that* badly," Preston said. But Ann knew he was only trying to be nice.

"It was a disaster!" she told him.

Preston sighed. "He'll come around. Trust me."

But she doubted it. As far as she could see, she had offended Jack Driscoll so badly that he was never going to forgive her.

Jack sat on a pile of hay in the large cage he used as a bed. He wondered if he'd get used to the stink of the hold by the time they reached their destination. He doubted it. The stench of the pile of dung left behind by a camel was the worst thing he'd ever had the misfortune to smell.

According to Choy, the sailor who had gotten him settled in his quarters, the crew sometimes captured animals and sold them. That explained the bottles of chloroform stacked against one wall. At least none of the animals was currently in residence. Jack had the place to himself.

"What have you got for me?" Carl asked as he entered the hold.

Scratch that. He only had the place to himself when Carl

wasn't down there checking up on him and the script. Jack stared down at the sheet of paper spooling out of his typewriter. "We're on the beach. The guy's been knifed. She stumbles backward as he sinks to his knees."

Carl's dark brown eyes gleamed. "That's great, Jack. He's on his knees, he's bleeding and? And?"

The ship rolled with a big wave. The cages rattled. Jack could feel his face turning green. He swallowed hard. "Ah, huh . . . yeah," was all he managed to say.

"Fend it off, Jack. You can make it to the end of the scene! Focus!"

Jack started to type. "Okay. She's staring at the body. It horrifies her. She's in shock."

Carl threw up his hands. "And she screams!" he exclaimed.

Jack dutifully typed in the scream, although he wasn't sure if Carl's star, Miss Ann Darrow, would be able to handle even that much acting. She was hardly more than a chorus girl. Why didn't Carl understand that?

"Compliments of Lumpy, the chef," Jimmy, the youngest of the sailors, called as he strode into the hold with two steaming bowls of gray slop. "Lambs' brains in cheese-and-walnut sauce."

Jack squeezed his eyes shut. He couldn't stand to look at the stuff, let alone eat it. Not with the waves rocking the ship—and his stomach. Jack wondered if even Lumpy—who was also the vet, the barber, the dentist, and chief medical officer—managed to eat his own cooking. He was so scrawny that Jack doubted it.

"Okay. She's screaming. He's sinking to his knees. There's blood everywhere, lots of blood." Carl practically rubbed his hands with glee. Jack was giving him good stuff, just the way Carl knew he would.

"That's not how it is. When a man's knifed in the back, there ain't much blood," Jimmy interrupted. "And he doesn't scream. The only sound he makes is a rush of air, like when you puncture a ball. He drops fast, like a stone. It's the shock."

"It's just a movie, kid," Jack told him.

"There's no such thing as a slow death, see?" Jimmy continued. "Not at the end. At the end it's always fast. The light in a man's eyes, one minute it's there, and then, it's gone. Nothing."

"Are you getting that, Jack?" Carl asked. Jack needed to get this stuff down. It was details like these that would make the script sing.

"Jimmy!"

Jimmy, Carl, and Jack all looked toward the voice. Hayes stood at the entrance to the hold. "You run those ropes up on deck like I told you?" Hayes asked.

According to Choy, Hayes was almost like a father to Jimmy. Choy had told Jack that Hayes had found Jimmy stowed away on the ship years before, half starved and beat up. The whole crew had basically adopted the kid, but Hayes especially had taken a liking to him.

Jimmy shot Hayes a nod and dashed up the stairs. Carl leaned over Jack's typewriter to make sure Jack had gotten down all of Jimmy's details about how a man looked when he was dying.

You shouldn't be worried about the script, Jack wanted to tell his buddy. You should be worried about your star. He doubted Ann Darrow knew how to do much more than fall on her behind to get a laugh.

Several weeks later, Jack couldn't believe he'd ever had a moment's doubt about Ann's acting ability. She was amazing. She could interpret his words better than any actress he'd ever worked with. The two of them had grown very close during the trip. He was amazed at how she'd managed to keep her sense of humor with the hard life she'd had, living all alone in the big city. Even now, as the only woman on the ship, she managed to make the most of their less-than-glamorous living conditions.

The whole crew had fallen in love with Ann—she had a knack for making everyone feel special. But Jack was fonder of her than anyone else, a fact that Carl would never let him forget.

As he and Carl took a walk around the deck a few nights later, Carl serenaded him with the tune "Falling in Love Again." It was clear that Carl thought Jack was falling in love with Ann. And maybe, just maybe, he was right.

"Here's to you!" Carl toasted Jack, with a big, happy grin on his face. Then the grin disappeared.

"Carl?" Jack asked. Something was very wrong.

"We're turning around!" Carl exclaimed. He immediately raced away from Jack and down to the ship's wheelhouse to find out why. "What's going on? Engelhorn! Why are we changing course?"

The captain handed Carl a cablegram. "It's from the bank. They're refusing to honor your check."

"Look, it's a stupid mistake!" Carl raked his fingers through his hair until it stood up in tufts. He knew it wasn't really a mistake; he had planned to give the captain a good check—just as soon as his movie was raking in the bucks.

"Outside!" Captain Engelhorn commanded. He shoved Carl back on deck. "There's a warrant out for your arrest. Did you know that? I have been ordered to divert to Rangoon."

Carl's face turned to ash. "Another week, that's all I'm asking. I haven't got a film yet. I've risked everything I have on this!"

"No, Carl, you risked everything *I* have," the captain corrected.

"What do you want? Tell me what you want. I'll give you anything!" Carl cried.

"I want you off my ship," Captain Engelhorn answered. And clearly he had nothing more to say.

Carl rushed back to Jack. He needed advice from his best friend. For the first time, he spilled out the story of the Norwegian skipper and the castaway and the island with the ancient civilization. He pulled out the map of Skull Island and slapped it into Jack's hand.

"I'm telling you, Jack, they're trying to get rid of me,"

Carl said. "They're gonna dump me in Rangoon and claim it for themselves."

"Claim *what*?" Jack asked. "Will you listen to yourself? You dragged us all out here on the pretext of making a movie!" The only thing that was completely clear to him was that his friend had been keeping secrets. Big ones.

Carl snatched the map away. "This *is* the movie! Do you have any idea how huge it could be? The last remnant of a dead civilization. It's gonna vanish, Jack!" He had to make his friend understand. "This island is sinking. It's gonna disappear from the face of the earth! Don't you get it?"

"No. No, I don't. You know why?" Jack asked. "You never told me, buddy . . . pal . . . friend!"

"That's right, I didn't," Carl replied. "You think I was born yesterday? I learned this business the hard way. No one had the guts to back me, so I backed myself."

"On the basis of what? A scrap of paper?" Jack shook his head.

"This island is real," Carl insisted. "It exists."

Jack took the map back and stared at it. "Maybe it does . . . and maybe it shouldn't be found." Something about the map caught his attention and he turned it so that the island appeared upside down. "What's that?"

"What?" Carl asked.

"There, that mark." Jack pointed.

"I dunno." Carl shrugged. "A coffee stain?"

Jack traced the dark image with his finger, and it became clear what the mark was.

The face of a gorilla.

"That's—" Carl began.

The low, funereal blast of the foghorn sounded from outside. The wind kicked up and blew the map out of Carl's hand and into the sea. *The Venture* was moving into a thick white fog that obscured everything.

Fog, Carl thought. *The castaway had mentioned fog like this in the story he told the Norwegian skipper!*

The ship slowed down. Feet slapped against the deck as the crew raced to their posts.

"Captain, do you know where you're going?" Hayes shouted.

Up in the crow's nest, Jimmy sprang to his feet. "Wall! There's a wall up ahead!"

He was right. Carl spotted a massive wall of dark gray stone stretching right out into the ocean. It rose two hundred feet into the air, making *The Venture* seem like a tiny toy boat in comparison.

"Cut the engines," Captain Engelhorn ordered from the wheelhouse.

But it was too late.

The Venture smashed into the stone wall with a sickening crunch.

2

Ann flew up the stairs and out onto the deck. She raced over to Carl and Jack. Together they stared at the crushed bow of *The Venture*.

"Rocks to starboard. To port. Rocks everywhere!" Jimmy cried from the crow's nest.

Jack stared through the mist. Jagged rocks surrounded the ship. They rose out of the water like stone claws, reaching out for *The Venture*.

"There's a clear spot! There's a gap!" Jimmy shouted.

The ship bucked under Ann's feet as the captain tried to steer through the reef of rocks. A moment later, the sound of metal against unforgiving stone ripped through her ears. For once, she couldn't think of anything to do or say to lighten a dark situation.

Jack cursed quietly as he realized that *The Venture* had run aground on the rocks. They were trapped. The damaged ship began spewing water in a dozen different places. Sailors leaped into action. Two of them hauled a mattress into place over one of the biggest leaks.

All Carl could do was stare at the island. He had to get over there. And it wasn't as if he could help repair *The Venture*. He was a filmmaker, not a sailor! He commandeered a few sailors and got his cast and crew loaded into the lifeboats. Finally, the moment was almost here. He was about to set foot on Skull Island!

The island was a dark chunk of land surrounded by the immense ocean. Jagged cliffs pierced the air. Crumbled remains of a civilization lay scattered on the crags of the beach—toppled statues, decaying idols. Above it all towered the incredibly tall stone wall that started out in the ocean and cut right across Skull Island. It divided the land mass in half.

As the lifeboats cut through the choppy water, Carl spotted faces appearing through the fog, frightening images carved in the stone wall—faces twenty feet high, frowning and grimacing. He made a mental note to get them on film.

Ann shivered at the sight of gruesome stone faces. It was as if they could see *The Venture* and the people onboard and were not happy that they were heading toward the island.

Jack reached for her hand to comfort her.

Carl couldn't be spooked. Everything he saw only added to his excitement about the film. He leaned so far forward that he was in danger of falling into the water, as if by leaning he could get them there faster. Preston looked a little nauseous as the small boat whipped back and forth in the rough sea. Bruce's lips moved as he rehearsed his lines, oblivious to the scenery around them. Jack's eyes flicked back and forth, trying to take everything in—the tiny patch of pebbles that made up the beach, the tall cliffs shooting straight up from it, the fragments of stone buildings, and the wall . . .

The giant wall that cast a dark shadow over them all.

The island grew bigger and bigger, as if it were moving toward the boats instead of the other way around. Below the surface of the water, giant stone faces—like the ones on the island—stared up at the sky. Their rock eyes were wide and blank. Their mouths gaped open, as if they were howling warnings to the people approaching Skull Island. Urging them to turn around. To go home and never come back.

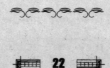

"Ann, position yourself under that carved head again," Carl told her.

She quickly moved into place. The juxtaposition of the massive, monstrous carving—so gruesome, it almost seemed to hold an evil spirit inside—and petite, beautiful Ann Darrow—the picture of innocence—was exactly what the director wanted.

Wind whistled through the stone ruins surrounding the cast and crew. The sound mixed with the crashing of the waves onto the shore. It was mournful and scary, and it set the perfect mood for the scene Carl had in mind.

"Ann . . . Look up slowly, Ann," he coached. "That's it. It scares you. You can't look away. You're helpless. You want to scream, but your throat's paralyzed."

Ann didn't find it hard to follow Carl's instructions. The sight of those empty stone eyes sucked all the saliva out of her mouth and made her throat feel as if it were packed with the pebbles that covered the beach.

"What does she think she's looking at?" Preston asked.

Carl ignored his assistant. "There's just one chance. Try to scream, Ann! Try!" he begged.

She let out a small, squeaky sound. The sound a paralyzed

throat would make. *Brilliant,* Carl thought.

"Now, throw your arms across your eyes and scream," he urged. "Scream, Ann. Scream for your life!"

Her blue eyes opened wide with terror, and Ann shrieked, long and high and loud. The sound felt as though it tore something inside her as it came out.

Then, something incredible happened. Something even Carl wasn't expecting.

Someone screamed back.

No, not someone. Some*thing.* Carl felt as if he'd been struck by lightning. That sound didn't come from anything human. It was so thunderous, it shook the trees. Birds exploded out of the trees and into the air. It was magnificent. And he'd gotten it all on film!

That scream made the hair on his arms and the back of his neck stand up. He could only imagine what it would do to a movie audience! Carl thought he might open his movie with the sound. Of course he'd need to scrap the story they had, but Carl was sure Jack could come up with some new stuff. The island had to come first. Carl was determined to be guided by what they found there. That would be his movie.

He was really hoping they'd discover the thing that

screamed back at Ann. He hurried in the direction of the bestial roar. "Herb, bring the camera!" he yelled.

An immense stone staircase—wide enough for five people to walk abreast—led off the beach and into the darkness of a vaulted tunnel. It was clearly an ancient entrance to whatever lay above. Carl strode toward the steep steps, many of them crumbling. He clearly expected the others to follow him.

Ann paused, gazing up the length of the dark stairs.

"Ann . . . ?" Jack asked, noticing her hesitation.

"I want to go back," she said softly.

"What is it?" he asked, his eyes dark with concern.

Ann continued to stare at the entrance to the tunnel. "I don't know!" All she knew was something up there felt . . . wrong.

"Carl!" Jack shouted.

Carl had already reached the entrance. "Jack—you're not gonna believe what's up here! It's incredible!"

"Hey! Wait up!" Jack called to Carl. He wasn't going to let his friend rush Ann into a situation that made her uncomfortable.

Carl turned around, a wide smile on his face. "I owe you, buddy. That goes for you, too, Ann. Herbert. Preston."

"Carl," Jack tried to interrupt.

"Sorry, Jack, I gotta say it. You believed in me. All of you. I wanna thank you for standing by the picture. It means so much to me—you saved my life." Carl swallowed hard. "I love you guys." He clapped his hands. "Ann—let's get a shot of you at the top of the stairs."

Ann nodded. She pushed down her unease and started up the staircase, careful to put her feet on parts of the steps that looked solid. The group followed, Bruce the last one in the line.

After Carl got his shot, the group continued under the stone arch and into the tunnel. The darkness grew deeper with each step they took.

"There's something on the ground up here," Mike said. "Something glittery." He leaned over and picked up the object that had caught his eye. He brushed the mud off it. "What is this?"

Then it became clear what it was, clear to everyone. The thing Mike held in his hand was a fragment of a jawbone. A *human* jawbone. It still had teeth. And one of the teeth was capped in gold. Ann wanted to look away, but couldn't.

"Great stuff!" Carl exclaimed. "See what I mean?

This film will be a masterpiece!"

As they continued on, Jack realized they were walking through a burial ground. They passed more bones. Mummies. Rotting tombs shaped like mouths with sharp, stone teeth jutting from the arched covers. Jack didn't understand why anyone would want to lay someone they loved to rest in a place like that.

"Are we very sure this is where we want to—" Bruce called from the back of the group.

"There's light up ahead," Preston interrupted. "Beautiful daylight."

Something inside Ann relaxed at the sight of the small patch of sun. She followed Carl and the others across a wobbly bamboo bridge that stretched across a section of the stairway with several missing stairs.

Carl held up one hand as he led the others out of the tunnel, cautioning everyone to keep quiet. Who knew what was out there?

What he saw in the sunlight was more of the same. A plateau stretched out in front of them. It was covered with bones. More deteriorating tombs and mausoleums. Some of them had been smashed open.

Ann shivered as her eyes adjusted to the light. The group was surrounded by death.

Beyond the tombs lay a ramshackle village of huts made from grass and bamboo. Their thin walls swayed in the wind. Pieces of their grass roofs were missing. Jack concluded they had clearly been made by people whose culture was much more primitive than the people who'd constructed the wall and the staircase and the carved faces.

The tremendous wall towered over the plateau—impenetrable rock that soared hundreds of feet into the air. A wide staircase ran through the village, right up to an enormous door in the wall. Two holes, like eyes, had been cut into the door, although the holes were covered by thick bars made of wood. Row upon row of sharpened bamboo spikes lined the top of the wall, as sharp as a carnivore's teeth.

"What are they keeping in there?" Preston whispered.

"What are they keeping *out?*" Jack whispered back.

A little girl appeared in front of Carl and the others. Her clothes were ragged. But it was her eyes that everyone looked at. The little girl had the eyes of a wild animal. Her body was painted with mud.

Carl pulled a Hershey's bar out of his pocket and offered it to the girl. "Look, chocolate. You like chocolate."

Rain began to fall. Carl ignored it. He took a step closer to the girl, waving the candy bar, ready to make friends. "Good to eat! Take it . . . take it!"

The girl stepped back. "Take it!" Carl took her by the wrist and tried to shove the Hershey's bar into her hand. If she took a bite of the candy, she'd understand that he'd only wanted to give her something she'd like.

"Carl, don't," Jack cautioned. The girl seemed almost rabid to him.

She cried out as she struggled to free herself from Carl's grip. At the sound of the little girl's squeal, villagers appeared. Old people, other children, women. They all stared at Carl, waiting to see what he would do.

Before Carl could make a decision, the little girl bit him on the wrist, drawing droplets of blood. He released her with a curse, and she darted away.

"Come on," Carl ordered the crew. "I want to get some footage of the village." He took a step forward. No one else moved. Uncertainty flickered across the faces of the film crew. "It's all right," Carl insisted. "It's just a bunch of women and kids and old people."

Mike lurched forward with his sound equipment, his movements awkward and jerky.

"Mike!" Ann cried.

He turned toward her, staring helplessly, tiny bubbles of foam appearing on his lips. Then he fell on his face—a notched, jagged spear stuck in his back.

Ann screamed, her eyes locked on the blood soaking into Mike's shirt.

"Rrroar." The thing, the creature behind the wall, roared back, just as it had the last time.

No one moved for a moment. Not Carl and his group. Not the islanders. The horrible, bestial cry had frozen them in place.

Then, as silent as fog, a new group of natives appeared. Men armed with clubs and spears. Their faces and bodies were painted with black mud. Jack's mind spun as he tried to come up with a plan, any kind of plan.

A woman appeared from the midst of the men. She stormed up to Ann and began to chant, her eyes burning with hatred. *"Larri yu sano korê . . . kweh yonê kah'weh ad larr . . . tôre Kông."* She stared accusingly at Ann, moving closer and grabbing Ann's arm as she chanted.

Ann could feel the woman's hot breath on her face. The woman's fingernails dug into Ann's skin. If Ann only knew what she wanted, she would give it to her, anything to get away from her horrible gaze.

The older villagers took up the woman's cry. *"Kong, Kong, Kong."* They rocked and wailed, as if they were possessed, mouths open, eyes wild with fear.

Pandemonium. Terror seized the natives and crew alike. Carl yelled at the villagers until one of the painted men grabbed him and threw him to the ground. Bruce struggled to free himself from two men with mud-streaked faces. Jack pulled Ann close to him, trying to shield her from the crazed woman. But another man rushed up and swung a club at Jack's head.

"Noooo!" Ann shrieked as Jack hit the ground.

The beast behind the wall echoed her cry.

Two of the villagers grabbed a sailor. Before anyone on the film crew could react, the sailor was forced down onto a rock. A club whistled through the air and came down on his neck, killing him.

Carl let out a howl of fury. He launched himself at the nearest villager and punched the man in the jaw.

But Carl wasn't in charge here. It didn't matter that he was the director of the movie. He was outnumbered by the angry islanders. Several of them grabbed Carl's arms and dragged him over to the stone where the dead sailor lay.

They pushed Carl's head down on the stone. The sailor's blood was still red and wet on the rock. One of the villagers raised his club. His mouth stretched open in a cry of triumph.

The club swung down.

And then a shot rang out. Loud and sudden.

Captain Engelhorn stepped from the darkness of the tunnel, a gang of sailors pouring out behind him. The captain raised his rifle and fired again. The man with the club toppled to the ground like a bowling pin hit by a ball moving at top speed. Then, more blood.

The captain rushed over and yanked Carl to his feet.

"Seen enough?" Engelhorn asked.

Carl's teeth were chattering together with fear, but he managed to get out the word.

"Yes."

"Lighten the ship! Anything that's not bolted down goes overboard!" Captain Engelhorn ordered the moment they were safely back on *The Venture*.

The crew sprang into action. After what had happened in the village, they all knew that they had to get away from this terrible island as fast as they could. But *The Venture* was still trapped on the rocks. The ship wouldn't be able to move until it was light enough to float over them.

Jimmy grabbed a chest and heaved it into the ocean. Two sailors threw a table overboard. Lumpy started hurling his pots and pans into the water. Carl spotted Choy snatching up the camera. "Not that! Stop!" Carl yelled, chasing after Choy. He yanked the camera away, but almost dropped it as the ship rocked under his feet. Choy made another grab for the heavy camera.

Captain Engelhorn strode over to the pair. "Throw that

thing overboard before I break your neck," he ordered Carl. "No more filming. No more pictures. Men have died because of you!"

"Don't threaten me. If you come any closer, I'll be compelled to defend myself," Carl warned him. Carl couldn't return to New York without his camera and the film. He had to finish his movie—or his life would be over. He'd spend the rest of his days in prison.

Engelhorn lunged for the camera, but Carl jerked away. The captain's face turned red with fury, and he swung his fist at Carl's head. Carl jumped backward just before the blow landed. But he lost his balance on the rolling deck, and the camera went flying.

Carl gave a grunt of frustration. He aimed a punch at Engelhorn's nose. The ship lurched, causing Carl's blow to go wide. He missed the captain by a foot. Recovering quickly, Carl punched Engelhorn in the gut, this time connecting. Engelhorn doubled over with an *ooof.* Before he could straighten up and go on the attack, an enormous wave swept over the deck railing and washed him off his feet.

Carl dropped to his knees and retrieved the camera.

He grinned in triumph even as he choked on a mouthful of saltwater.

The ship gave another great heave as it broke free from the rocks. They were floating. They were free of Skull Island!

Engelhorn leaped to his feet. "Start the main engines!" he yelled.

Up in the wheelhouse, Hayes followed the command. He fired up the engines and steered *The Venture* out to sea.

All around the ship, sailors cheered and whooped with relief.

"Stop! Turn back!" Jack's voice broke into the cheering. He climbed up from below deck and ran to the captain. "We have to turn back. They've taken Ann!"

The ship was rolling and tossing all around Ann as she huddled in her cabin. She couldn't stop trembling. She pulled her silk robe tightly around her, but it didn't help. She'd gotten wet and chilled in the lifeboat as the sailors rowed back to *The Venture,* but now, even though she had changed into dry clothes, she continued to shiver.

It was her spirit that was cold. She kept thinking of how Mike had stared at her the second before he fell down dead.

And that poor sailor who'd been killed. All that blood . . .

A wave slapped against the porthole, loud as thunder, and Ann jumped. The ship heaved, and her closet door swung open, spewing movie costumes onto the floor. She knelt to retrieve them, and saw the doorknob to the cabin turn.

Ann scrambled to her feet. The cabin door flew open. One of the men from the village stood there. The mud on his face was streaked with water, making him look even more terrifying than the men she'd seen on the island.

Before Ann could scream, he clamped one of his hands down over her mouth. Was he going to kill her? He wrapped a strong arm around her body and dragged her down the dark, narrow corridor. Ann prayed someone would see them, but he pulled her out onto the lower deck and over the rail so swiftly that there was no time for any help to arrive.

Seawater filled Ann's mouth and nose, and then ran down her throat. The islander tightened his grip on her as he took hold of a rope he'd secured to *The Venture*. His arm pressed hard against Ann's throat as they were both towed through the ocean. More villagers stood on the shore, pulling on the rope that was hauling Ann and her captor back to Skull Island.

Ann had no idea what the people of the island wanted. But when they yanked her onto the tiny beach, she saw that she was the only person who had been taken from *The Venture*. Her heart gave a lurch. Had anyone even realized she was no longer onboard?

There was no time to think, no time to plan an escape. The islanders dragged Ann up the wide staircase, through that horrible tunnel, and back to where Mike had been murdered.

Men thronged the center of the village. There must have been at least one hundred of them. As soon as the other villagers caught sight of her, they began to chant again. *"Kong, Kong, Kong."* Ann wished that she could understand their language. What was Kong? What did Kong have to do with her?

A woman came forward and looped a necklace around Ann's throat. It was made of ten-inch-long thorns, with what Ann thought were tiny bird skulls strung amid the barbs. It felt heavy around Ann's neck, and one of the thorns pressed into her flesh. Two men grabbed her arms and forced her over to the stone wall, the wall that towered over the huts of the village. Torches now blazed high up on top of it. Burning oil ran down the sides in several places—a liquid fire that coursed behind the massive carved faces, making their eyes and open mouths glow in a terrifying spectacle. When Ann looked at them, she felt as if a giant hand had reached into her body and squeezed.

Ann's captors pointed to the steep stone staircase that led to the top. She had no choice but to climb. She was afraid that if she didn't, she would end up dead like that sailor, with her head bashed in.

So she began to climb. It took a long time to make it all the way to the top of the twenty-story-high wall. By the time Ann put her foot onto the final step, her legs felt numb with exhaustion, her mind numb with fear. Two men, faces smeared with mud, grabbed her and pulled her over the top of the wall and onto a wooden contraption. They moved quickly, their eyes wild. They seemed as frightened as Ann felt.

The men tied Ann's wrists to the arm of what looked like a huge crane made of tree trunks lashed together with thick vines.

"What are you doing? What do you want from me?" she cried, even though she knew they did not share a language.

Drums began to beat. Men on the wall and men on the ground pounded on them faster and faster. *"Kong! Kong!*

Kong!" the other islanders shrieked along with the *boom! boom! boom!*

Ann's wooden trap began to move, jerking her toward the edge of the wall. She dug in her heels. The jungle vegetation on the other side of the wall was thick and wild, dense enough to hide . . . anything. Ann didn't want to end up down there.

But she had no say in the matter. The men on top of the wall were letting out a rope attached to her wooden prison. They let out more rope, and the crane jerked forward again. Ann's feet left the stone of the wall. The muscles in her arms spasmed as they took her full weight. She swung out into the air, hanging by the vines around her wrists, her legs dangling. Ann let out a terrified scream. She had never felt more helpless.

The crane was still moving, swinging her farther out over the jungle. Then it began to lower her down, placing her on top of a tall outcropping of rock. It was a relief for Ann to have her feet on solid ground again—until she saw the skulls on the spikes surrounding her. Human skulls. Ann gasped with terror. She realized that she stood on some sort of altar, far from help. The wooden crane had become a bridge to this altar—a bridge she couldn't hope to cross back to the village.

The men on top of the wall continued to chant and drum, staring down at Ann. *"Kong, Kong, Kong!"* She could hear the women and children shouting from the other side of the wall.

The ground began to shake. It was as if the earth were a huge drum and a giant were beating on it. Ann strained against the vines that held her captive, pulling and twisting with all her strength. Her wrists started to bleed, but the vines wouldn't break.

A flock of birds burst out of the trees to her left. Ann jerked her head toward the motion. Something was moving through the jungle toward her, but the smoke from the torches made it hard to see.

The ground shook harder. Ann would have fallen if the vines hadn't held her upright.

A gust of wind momentarily cleared the smoke. She saw a foot. A huge, leathery foot. Then Ann raised her eyes up and up and up. She screamed. Her throat felt as if it was being ripped to shreds, but she couldn't stop.

A gorilla crouched in front of her, its knuckles scraping the ground. It was massive. Unnaturally huge. Its yellow eyes were the size of automobile tires. It stared down at Ann.

Then it reared up to its full height. It stood twenty-five feet high at least.

The creature beat its chest with its mammoth fists and let out a roar.

It was the roar Ann had heard on the beach. And in the village. This was the creature who had answered her before, and now it had come to claim its prize.

The gorilla reached for Ann. Then everything went black.

4

Carl glanced from the fires he saw burning on the island to Captain Engelhorn's face. What would his decision be? Carl couldn't force him to stop the ship and allow his crew to go back for Ann. Engelhorn held all the cards in this situation. And that made Carl crazy.

The sailors gathered on deck, waiting for a word from the captain. They all loved Ann. Carl knew they wanted to go after her.

"Captain?" Hayes asked at last, breaking the silence.

Captain Engelhorn narrowed his eyes as he stared at the fiery orange glow over Skull Island. He gave a curt nod.

"All hands going ashore report to stations! Jump to it!" Hayes barked.

The crew leaped into action. Some of the men swung two lifeboats out away from the ship and lowered them into the water. Others threw guns and equipment into the boats.

Carl thrust the camera into Herb's arms and ordered Preston to help him get it into one of the boats without the captain noticing. He thought about asking Jack to help, too, but Jack was busy loading boxes of ammo—what looked like enough ammo to kill everything on the island.

Carl climbed into the lifeboat Preston and Herb had chosen, and the sailors started rowing through the rough water. He had to find Ann! He had to find his star!

The boats landed on the tiny beach, and the group raced back up the staircase. The steps' landings were almost vertical, and Carl's heart felt ready to pound out of his chest. But he kept pace with the captain and Jack at the front of the group. They all had to slow down a little in the darkness of the tunnel or risk breaking their necks, but in minutes the group broke out onto the plateau.

The rivers of fire flowing down the mammoth wall gave Carl, Jack, and the other men enough light to see by. The entire village was filled with shrieking islanders. They pounded on drums and chanted, all of them staring at the wall. The sailors fired warning shots, and the villagers scattered.

"Help!" Ann screeched from the other side of the wall. Jack could feel her horror in his own body. Then again came an echoing wild roar, as if in response to Ann's scream.

"What in God's name was that?" Captain Engelhorn cried.

No one answered. No one knew what it was. Jack led the party over to the base of the towering wall. He immediately began to climb the stone staircase, trying to get to the top. Carl spotted a break in the wall. A giant wooden gate—as tall as the wall itself and looking like a face with eyes—filled the gap. He tore over to it and peered through an opening between the poles. And there he saw Ann. She was clasped in the hand of the most amazing creature he had ever laid eyes on. It looked like a gorilla, but this was no ordinary gorilla. It was massive, at least four times larger than any creature Carl had ever seen.

He'd thought Ann and Bruce were his stars. But that creature would be the true star of Carl's movie, if he could capture it on film. Clutching Ann, the beast retreated into the jungle.

"She's gone!" Jack yelled from the top of the wall. He scrambled down the crumbling staircase. "She's gone," he repeated breathlessly.

Carl knew she was gone. He'd seen the thing that took her.

Jack stared at his friend, and he sensed that Carl was

holding something back. "You saw something, Carl," he said.

"She was taken by an ape," Carl said. It was the easiest explanation.

"What kind of ape?" Jack asked, alarmed.

"I don't know," Carl replied. It was the truth. It didn't resemble any ape he'd ever seen before.

"A gorilla?" Engelhorn asked, as he handed out tommy guns to his crew.

"I couldn't see. Too dark," Carl told him.

"What does it matter?" Lumpy cried. "One bloody monkey is as good as the next!"

But he hadn't seen what Carl had seen. Carl knew this was no "monkey."

"Who's coming?" Jack asked. He strode up to the huge bamboo gate and grabbed it with both hands. He grunted as he tried to tear the thing down.

"Step aside," Hayes told him, his voice grim. He aimed one of the machine guns at the wood and blasted a section of the enormous gate to smithereens. Then Hayes handed the gun to Jack. Jimmy loaded a rifle.

Hayes shook his head. "Not you, Jimmy." He held out his hand for the weapon.

"Come on, Mr. Hayes, look at them," Jimmy argued,

gesturing to Carl, Herb, Bruce, and Jack. "None of them knows which way to point a gun. You need me. Miss Darrow needs me."

Jimmy was right. Jack was a great writer, but he knew nothing about weapons. Herb was a genius with a camera, but that was it. Bruce Baxter only knew how to pretend to shoot. Carl was the director, and he had never held a gun in his life.

But Hayes didn't seem to understand that. He snatched the gun from Jimmy's hands. "She needs you coming after her with this thing like she needs a hole in the head. You're staying here."

Jimmy's face fell. Carl stayed out of it. He let Hayes figure out who was coming and what weapons to bring. He turned his attention to Herb and Preston. "Bring the tripod and all of the film stock," Carl instructed them.

"You wanna go with the six-inch lens?" Herb asked.

Carl considered it. "No, the wide angle should do just fine. But—"

"This is a rescue mission, Mr. Denham," Engelhorn interrupted.

"Correct, Mr. Engelhorn," Carl answered. "I am fully

committed to saving Miss Darrow . . . and whatever is left of my failing career." He needed to make this movie. If he didn't, no one would ever give him the money to make another one. The investors would have him arrested and thrown into jail. He'd be finished for good. This was Carl's last chance.

Engelhorn's lips tightened, but he didn't argue. "You got guns, you got food, you got ammo," he snapped. "You got twelve of my men, including Lumpy, Choy, and Hayes. And you got twenty-four hours."

Bruce swallowed so hard, Carl could hear it from several feet away. "Twenty-four hours?" he repeated.

"This time tomorrow we haul anchor," the captain answered.

"Let's go," Jack said. He wasn't willing to wait another second to start searching for Ann. They'd lost too much time flapping their lips already. He stepped through the hole Hayes had blasted in the mammoth gate. The rest of the men followed him.

They made their way into the jungle. The trees had vines as thick as a man's wrist twisting around their trunks. The undergrowth came up to Jack's shoulders. Moss covered everything—every rock, every tree, and most of the ground. Steam rose from the earth.

It was like another world.

Herb limped behind Carl. He'd lost a leg on another one of Carl's movies when a sea lion had bitten it off. And his fake leg wasn't comfortable when he had to walk very far. Carl loved the guy for sticking with him on every movie despite that.

"I want shots of all of this," Carl told him. "Make sure you get that steam coming up from the swamps. And shoot some of those tree branches that look like twisted hands. Great stuff!"

Jack shot Carl a look that would have killed him, if looks really could kill. Clearly, he didn't think Carl could shoot a film and rescue Ann at the same time. Carl was sure he could.

Choy stopped so suddenly, Carl almost bumped into him. Carl realized Hayes had signaled the group to a halt. A moment later, he found out why. Something was coming toward them. Was it the ape?

The sailors raised their guns. They shot in every direction. *Bam, bam, bam!*

"Cut it out! Hold your fire!" Hayes yelled. He led the

way into a clearing up ahead. He lit a flare, coloring the open space with a red glow.

Thud!

A huge creature fell to the ground in front of them.

Carl jerked his head toward Herb to make sure he was still filming. He was, good man.

Then he turned back to study the beast. It looked like a dinosaur. An actual prehistoric creature—but how could that be? Its mottled brown body lay so close that Carl could reach down and touch one of the spikes running down its back if he wanted to.

"Ligocristus," Lumpy muttered. "It's a ligocristus. An actual ligocristus."

The ground began to shake. Another dinosaur charged out of the jungle and thundered across the clearing. Blood gushed from its side—one of the sailors had made a direct hit with a shot from the tommy gun—and the wound had made it half crazy. It bellowed out a death cry as it staggered toward the men. Then its tail whipped out—and knocked three sailors to the ground.

Hayes raised his gun and shot the beast in the eye. Blood spattered across the large crest on its head. Jack stood so close, he could smell the coppery scent of it. The earth shuddered as the creature crashed to the ground next to the other dinosaur.

"Aren't these things supposed to be extinct?" Preston asked, his voice little more than a squeak.

Lumpy spit. "They are now."

Bruce slowly backed away from the dead creatures. "What kind of place is this?" he asked.

Carl knew the answer. It was a place where anything could happen. He couldn't wait to see what they would find next.

Ann's eyes fluttered open. For a moment she couldn't remember where she was. The green floor of a forest sped by twenty feet below her and it all came rushing back—Skull Island. The fiery village. The giant ape. He clutched her in his hand as he traveled through the jungle. The creature moved much faster—and more gracefully—than she would have thought possible for a being of his size.

What chance did she have against an animal of such speed and power? She must have seemed to the creature as a rabbit would seem to a hunting dog. Soft and small—and very easy to kill.

Terror rushed through her, along with a million questions. Where was this monster taking her? What did he want of her? Why had the villagers—

All questions flew out of Ann's head as the beast came to a stop in an open patch of rocky ground. She felt his eyes boring into her, and she forced herself to look into his face.

All the breath escaped from Ann's lungs at the sight. A long, yellow fang jutted over the ape's bottom lip. That one tooth was larger than the clubs the villagers had used to kill the sailor. Ann knew he could rip her in half with one casual motion.

She studied the rest of the beast's face. It looked like it belonged to a prizefighter, with its crooked jaw, its torn ear, and crisscrossing flesh-colored scars. A mangled eyelid drooped over a huge yellow eye.

Maybe he can't see well from that eye, Ann thought. *Can I use that to my advantage?*

Hope flared inside her—then sputtered out. It was insanity to think about escape when she was being held tightly in a hand that was almost as big as her apartment in New York City.

The ape grunted. He twitched his hand, and Ann plunged through the air until she hung upside down, her feet held between two huge fingers. Her blond hair tumbled across her face, and the necklace the natives had forced around her neck fell to the ground.

It landed on top of a pile of identical necklaces, necklaces mixed in with bones. They looked like pickup sticks alongside the ape's huge feet. But they were bones. Human bones.

Ann's body convulsed with fear. Obviously, there had been many others before her. And all were dead now. Ann kicked and flailed, trying to pull away from the ape's hand. She screamed—a mix of fear and fury.

It made the beast angry. He snarled and raised Ann to his face. His fingers loosened slightly as he brought her to his mouth. To the humongous yellow teeth. Ann jerked away with all her strength and hurled herself out into the air. Sparks of light exploded in front of her eyes as she landed on the bones below, snapping a few with the force of her fall. The ape roared with frustration. The vibrations ripped through Ann as she scrambled to her feet and bolted for the jungle. She had to get out of the open and into the cover of the trees.

Vines caught at her feet as she ran, each vine as thick as her arm. The trees here were huge, just like the ape. Most of them were more than fifty feet tall. She couldn't see a way out of the jungle, but she had to keep running. *Don't let me trip, don't let me trip,* she silently pleaded. Her lungs felt as if they had caught fire, and her legs felt as if the bones had been stripped from them—but she didn't allow herself to slow down.

The beast ran after her. The ground shuddered under the weight of his feet with every step. Ann heard trees crashing down as the ape mowed through the jungle.

She hit a slope, and she couldn't slow down fast enough. With a cry, Ann fell to the ground and rolled. As she struggled back to her feet, a gunshot echoed through the jungle. It was the most beautiful sound she'd ever heard.

The islanders didn't have guns. It had to be men from *The Venture*. A rescue party was nearby! "Help!" Ann shouted. She ran in the direction the shot had come from, struggling to keep on her feet on the steep downhill slope. "Help!"

"Ann! Ann, over here!" Jack yelled back.

Jack. Jack had come after her. The sound of his voice gave her extra strength. Ann lengthened her stride, running faster than she ever had.

Crash!

A tree fell to the ground, creating a wall on one side of Ann. The ape roared with triumph. He was close, so close.

All she could do was run—and hope that she would

reach Jack before the beast reached her.

A broken tree flew over her head and landed in her path with a world-rocking thud. She veered and kept running. She lost her footing again, but didn't let the fall stop her for more than an instant. She felt the soft earth turn to rock under her feet.

Just in time, Ann realized that the rock was about to turn to thin air! She skidded to a stop, her heart thundering against her ribs. A valley shrouded by mist lay far below her. One more step and she would have fallen to her death.

"Jack!" she screeched. Where was he?

She heard motion in the underbrush behind her.

Ann whipped around. The mighty ape loomed above her. There was nowhere to run.

He snatched Ann up in his fist. She was his captive again.

"Jack!" Ann's terrified scream rang through the immense forest of Skull Island.

A lump formed in Jack's throat. She was calling for him. She needed his help!

He spun toward the sound of Ann's voice and ran, the others in the rescue party only steps behind him. But he made no headway through the dense undergrowth. It was as if the jungle wanted to stop him from reaching her. Long vines snaked down in front of his face, making it hard to see. Tangled, twisted roots slid out of the ground, grabbing at his feet. And gigantic stone columns, slick with moss, seemed to pop out of nowhere to block his path.

"Ann!" he shouted, frustrated. "Ann!"

The beast, the ape that Denham had seen, roared in answer. The sound sent an arrow of cold from Jack's neck down to the pit of his stomach. The thing sounded enraged. Ann screamed again, and it echoed through the trees. Then she fell silent.

The silence was worse than her shrieks had been.

Jack thrashed through the plants, using every ounce of energy he had to reach her. Beyond one final branch, he could see a clearing. He shoved the branch to the side and jerked to a stop. In front of him, a waterfall spewed from the mouth of a gruesome face carved into a dark cliff. A pile of spiked necklaces lay to one side of the small rocky clearing.

The one on top had a clump of blond hair tangled in its long, sharp thorns.

Jack's stomach cramped as he looked at it. Slowly, not

quite wanting to get there, he walked over and picked up the necklace. Yes, the long blond hair was Ann's.

"It's a bleeding boneyard!" Lumpy spat out as he and the others raced up next to Jack.

Jack let his eyes move over the clearing. Human bones lay scattered everywhere. "Ann! Ann!" he shouted.

There was no answer.

Carl checked to make sure Herb was filming the bones. They lay scattered about, as if the bodies had been torn limb from limb. Jack noticed Carl staring at a huge gash cut through the forest—trees and plants trampled and pushed to the sides to create a path. What kind of beast could have caused such damage?

Jack had a feeling that Carl knew.

"Jeez, Jimmy," Hayes suddenly said from across the clearing. Jack turned to see *The Venture*'s second in command facing off with Jimmy. Hayes didn't look happy to see the kid out in the jungle—he'd told Jimmy to stay in the village. Hayes thought of Jimmy like a son.

"Turn around, pretend you didn't see me," Jimmy begged.

"You aren't supposed to be here." Hayes grabbed Jimmy's gun away.

"I need that," Jimmy protested.

"I'm not giving you a gun!" Hayes snarled.

"You were younger than me when they gave you one," Jimmy shot back. Hayes had fought with the Harlem Hellfighters in World War I and received a Croix de Guerre.

Hayes and Jimmy stared at each other in a silent battle of wills.

Jack turned away, not wanting to get in the middle. Carl was still staring at the wide swath beaten through the jungle. "What took her, Carl?" he asked.

"I told you it was dark," Carl replied.

"I know you're lying," Jack snapped. "I just don't understand why."

"Please, Mr. Hayes! I wanna help bring her back!" Jimmy exclaimed loudly from across the clearing.

"That's what we all want, kid," Carl called, turning his back on Jack.

"Ain't gonna be much to bring back, if you ask me," Lumpy muttered, staring down at all the bones.

"No one asked you," Jack said.

"Come on, fellas, we all want the same thing," Carl cried. "To see Miss Darrow's safe return . . . isn't that why we're here?"

The members of the rescue party exchanged worried glances. Several of them nodded.

Hayes threw a gun to Jimmy. "You heard the man. Get moving."

6

At least the sun is up now, Jack thought. *That should help us find Ann.* Not that it took a lot of light to follow the path the ape—as Carl called whatever had captured Ann—took through the jungle. The trail was so wide that it looked as if a couple of tanks had cleared the way.

Jack knew they weren't tracking any ape. He wished he could grab Carl by the neck and shake the truth out of him. But he had more important things to do. Ann's last scream kept replaying in his mind. They didn't have much time to rescue her.

"I'm knackered. Gotta have a breather," Lumpy announced. They'd just entered a narrow valley with sheer cliffs rising up on either side.

"We don't have time for this. We've already lost too much ground," Jack protested. But the other sailors plopped down on the grass next to Lumpy. "Come on, get up," he urged them. Every muscle in his body was tensed, ready to continue the hunt for Ann.

"They're not about to quit on you. Cut them some slack," Hayes told him. He turned toward the men. "All right, you got five minutes."

Jack sighed, frustrated. Five minutes. Didn't Hayes realize what could happen to Ann in five minutes? But nobody backed him up. Carl and Preston actually got the camera set up on a tripod.

"Bruce, over here!" Carl called. "I want to get a wide shot of the valley with you in it."

Preston frowned. "Carl, shouldn't we think about conserving film stock? I mean, we're gonna want to finish Miss Darrow's scenes . . . when we get her back. So my thought is to save what we have and temporarily stop photography."

Jack snorted. He couldn't believe they were still talking about the stupid movie.

"You want me to stop shooting?" Carl sounded shocked.

"It's a plan," Preston replied. "What do you think?"

"Preston, let me tell you something. All you know about movies, you could stick in a cat's behind." Carl turned to Herb. "You got the shot?"

Herb nodded, and Carl led them up the hill, heading out of the valley.

Jack stayed with the sailors. He had no interest in Carl Denham and his movie. Not anymore. "You better be back by the time this break is over!" he called after them. Carl ignored him, but Preston waved without looking back.

Jack knew he should probably sit down with the sailors. Get a little rest. But he was too worried about Ann. He paced around the valley. Out here it was harder to figure out which way the thing had taken her. There were no trees to knock over, just open grassland. He stumbled a little as he accidentally stepped into a deep depression. Then he backed up, trying to figure out what it was. His heart skipped a beat when the answer came to him.

A footprint.

"Get over here!" Jack called to the sailors. "You've got to see this."

Lumpy reached him first. "Bloody Nora!" he burst out.

"Did the thing that took Miss Ann make that?" Jimmy asked.

"There's only one creature capable of leaving a print that size . . . the abominable snowman," Lumpy answered. "And I, for one, have no desire to meet it face-to-face. Believe me, fellas, against something this big, we got no chance." The other sailors muttered in agreement.

Jack couldn't take his eyes off the print. It did look the right shape to have been made by an ape. But the size . . . The size . . .

"The animal that made that has to be . . . what? Twenty, twenty-five feet?" Hayes said quietly, coming up next to Jack.

"Carl saw it. Let's ask him," Jack said.

"Where did he go, anyway?" Hayes asked.

Jack pointed up the hill . . . and saw Bruce running down it. "What's wrong?" he yelled to the actor.

"Carl found . . . He's—he's—um. He wanted me to—but I . . . ," Bruce stammered.

His voice was drowned out by a sound like thunder. The ground began to shake, as if a stampede was pounding toward them. Jack heard Herb screaming, a high, shrill shriek of pure horror.

Jack jerked his head toward the sound and saw Carl and Herb being chased back into the valley by a herd of brontosaurs. Living, breathing, *running* brontosaurs. The dinosaurs' legs were as thick as the trunks of redwoods. Their necks had to be at least twenty feet long. It was hard to believe they could move that fast without their necks breaking.

"Run!" Hayes yelled.

Jack ran. The other sailors were already sprinting away. Carl tore past, lugging the heavy camera and its stand.

He stumbled and dropped the camera.

"Leave it!" Jack shouted.

"No!" Carl shouted back. He bent to pick up the camera even though the dinosaurs were about to crush him.

Jack grabbed him by the arm, ready to pull him out of the way. As he looked back at the charging herd, he noticed another breed of dinosaurs. Suddenly Jack understood why the brontosaurs were stampeding—they were being chased. Hunted. These new dinosaurs made the brontosaurs look like house pets.

Their huge fangs dripped with saliva. A row of spikes like gigantic teeth ran along their backs. Their heads were huge, out of proportion to their bodies—and all he could see of their heads was mouth. They raced along on two tremendously powerful legs, much faster than the brontos.

Carnotaurs. The name popped into Jack's head. He'd read about them at the American Museum of Natural History. They were carnivorous and brutal, one of the most dangerous dinosaurs.

He yanked Carl to his feet. The director managed to grab

the camera and its tripod, and they raced after the others. Jack hoped the carnotaurs would be more interested in the brontosaurs than they were in humans. But it didn't matter. Even if the carnotaurs didn't try to eat them, the brontosaurs could crush them like ants. And they were right behind Jack and the group of sailors, their enormous feet coming closer every second.

Then the brontosaurs were all around them, the sound of the stampede drowning out everything else. Massive feet slammed into the ground on all sides, each one at least a couple of yards wide. The huge dinosaurs were terrified, racing for their lives. They ran erratically, veering from side to side, so that it was impossible to tell where their feet would land next. In front of Jack, one of the sailors tripped, fell, and was instantly trampled. Another man wove his way out of the sea of dinosaur legs—and was instantly snatched up in the teeth of a carnotaur.

"If we stay inside the herd of brontos, we're safer!" Jack shouted to Carl.

Bruce dashed toward the front of the herd, sprinting hard until he got out in front of all the dinosaurs. It was like one of his movies. He spun to face the dinosaurs and aimed at a carnotaur with his tommy gun. Bad idea.

"No!" Jack shouted.

Bruce fired. A bronto to Jack's right staggered, hit by Bruce's wild shot. Then, with a bellow, the brontosaur collapsed—cartwheeling into the rest of the herd. Its long neck and tail thrashed about violently, smashing one sailor into the grass. Another brontosaur crashed into the one who had fallen. Then another. They were like dominoes made of flesh. Men screamed as they were caught underneath the downed brontosaurs.

Two of the carnotaurs thundered over to the brontosaurs that lay helpless on the ground and began to feast on them. Out of the corner of his eye, Jack saw one of the predators turn toward him. He sped away as fast as could, his heart about to burst with the exertion. But the carnotaur came after him, every stride it took matching ten of Jack's. It would catch him in a matter of seconds.

There was no possibility he could outrun the carnotaur. There was no place to hide. It was over.

Then a shot rang out. With a loud bellow, the beast behind him collapsed.

Jack raised his eyes to the shooter. Hayes. He'd just saved Jack's life.

"Go, go, go!" Hayes yelled. He picked off three more

carnos with his gun, one after the other. But more kept coming. The men had to get away.

The only way out of the steep valley was to run straight to the end—but the carnotaurs would definitely catch them before then. Their only chance was to try to climb straight up the sheer cliff on the side of the valley. Jack veered over to the wall and started up. The others followed. His shoes slipped on the slimy moss, and he slid back down a few feet. He continued up in a crouch, using rocks and weeds and vines as handholds. The other members of the rescue party climbed with him, all of them panting with the effort.

Four carnotaurs split from the herd of brontosaurs and sped toward the rescue party. Even with their deadly claws, they had to struggle to scale the cliff. One of the sailors in front of Jack lost his grip on the weed he was using to pull himself up. He fell from the wall with a terrified cry. Jack tried to grab him. But the sailor slithered past him, then right between two carnotaurs—and into the waiting mouth of a third.

The sound of the man's bones cracking in the powerful jaws made Jack feel sick. There was nothing he could do for the sailor. So he continued to climb. He spotted a narrow crack in the rocks above him. Hayes and a few others were already heading toward it. The fissure was wide enough for the men to squeeze through, but the huge carnotaurs wouldn't fit. If they could reach that crack, it would save their lives.

"Herb, come on!" Carl yelled. He shot a look over his shoulder. Herb had fallen behind. His bad leg slowed him down. Carl found a foothold on top of a boulder, and then leaned down, trying to reach him. "Come on, Herb." He lowered the tripod toward the cameraman. "Do as I say! Grab it!"

Herb reached for the tripod, his fingers grasping the very end of a pole. Carl felt a rush of relief. Then Herb's fake leg gave way beneath him. He fell backward, too far away for Carl to help him. Herb rolled into the path of an oncoming carnotaur. Carl spun back toward the rock—he couldn't watch what happened next. Herb was a good man, and Carl didn't want to see him die. He tried not to listen to the horrifying sounds behind him as he kept climbing. Finally he reached the crack. It was tight, just a narrow fissure in the rock. Jack climbed through and pulled Carl in behind him, the jagged stone of the walls biting into their skin.

Hayes, Bruce, Jimmy, Lumpy, and Choy were already inside. Carl scrambled after them through the narrow stone passage and out to the other side.

No carnotaurs. No brontosaurs. No dinosaurs of any kind. They stood in an empty clearing with a swamp off to one side. Dazed, Carl stared back at the fissure they'd crawled through. He couldn't believe Herb was gone.

Jack took a deep breath. The steam rising from the swamp smelled almost as bad as the camel dung back on the ship. But he didn't care. He sucked in a big lungful of the stinking air. He was alive!

Now all he had to do was find Ann.

After a moment of silence and breath catching, Hayes took charge. "Do a head count," he ordered the closest sailor. "I wanna know how many injured and how bad."

Lumpy gave a harsh laugh. "Injured? Four of us are dead!"

Carl finally dropped his camera. He took a swig from the silver flask he always carried. His hands shook. He'd known Herb for a long time. Preston walked over and touched his arm. "Carl?" he said softly.

"What are we doing here, Preston? How could it end like this?" Carl took another pull on his flask.

Preston didn't answer.

Jack turned to Hayes. "How much rope have we got?" he asked, eyeballing the width of the swamp.

"Are you out of your mind?" Lumpy cried. "We can't get across! Forget this! I'm off!" He strode away from the group.

"He's got a point," Bruce said slowly. "Engelhorn sails in nine hours . . ."

"So?" Jimmy burst out. "We have to save Miss Darrow."

"Didn't you hear me?" Bruce asked. "We're gonna be stranded here!"

"I heard you—and I ain't going back!" Jimmy snapped.

"Yeah?" Lumpy called from several feet away. "Well, you were never destined to have a long and happy life."

"Shut it!" Hayes ordered.

Bruce made his way over to Jimmy. "She's dead," he said firmly. "Miss Darrow was a great girl, no question. A wonderful person. We're all gonna miss her."

Jack felt like punching him. How could he even think of giving up the search for Ann? "I always knew you were nothing like the tough guy you play on screen," he spat out. "I just never figured you for a coward."

"Hey, pal, wake up! I'm an actor," Bruce answered. "Heroes don't look like me, not in real life. In real life they got bad teeth, bald spots, and beer guts. They're normal!"

"Are you done?" Jack demanded.

"Yes, I am," Bruce said, eyes dark with fury—and fear. "Go ahead, make me the bad guy. I've played them before and let me tell you what I learned. There are no bad guys, only bad writers."

He slung his gun over his shoulder and stomped over to join Lumpy.

"Anyone else?" Hayes asked.

A few other sailors joined the cowards who wanted to abandon Ann.

"Come on, Choy. Don't be an imbecile," Lumpy called.

"Not me, I stay with the boys. I got Charlie Atlas training. I complete the course." Choy flexed his arm. His bicep muscle didn't move. "Perfect manhood very hard to kill," he added.

Carl sighed. "I think I lost my way," he said. "Somewhere back there, we took a wrong turn."

"It's not your fault what happened to Herb. It's no one's fault," Preston said.

Carl straightened his shoulders, the usual gleam returning to his eyes. "Herbert didn't die for nothing," he said slowly. "He died for what he believed in and I'm gonna honor that. He died believing there is still some mystery left in this world. And we can all have a piece of it, for the price of an admission ticket." Carl got to his feet and addressed Bruce and the other men who wanted to leave. "We're gonna finish this film for Herb and donate the proceeds to his wife and kids."

Jack gave a sigh of relief. Bruce thought about it, and then nodded. He led the others back to the main group. The search for Ann would continue.

Preston smiled. "That's fantastic!"

"Here's to the motion picture business!" Carl drained his flask. "The greatest fantasy of all!"

Ann bounced around in the giant ape's hand as he bounded across chasms and leaped over rivers. The beast moved too fast for her to get any real sense of what was around her. Splotches of brown and blue and green flew past, making her dizzy.

She struggled to wrap her arms around the closest of the ape's fingers. But she couldn't anchor herself. She flopped back and forth across the creases in his palm as if she were a rag doll. With each step he took, she moved farther away from Jack. Farther away from hope.

A ferocious growl jolted her from her dazed state. It hadn't come from the ape. Ann struggled again to steady herself so she could get a good look. She saw a brief flash of something huge and reptilian lunging toward her.

Snap!

A giant pair of jaws bit into the ape's wrist, just a few

feet away from Ann. The ape howled in pain and anger. Hot saliva splashed over Ann's body as another creature attacked, using its gigantic jagged teeth to latch onto the ape. The creatures had teeth like axes and sharp horns on their heads. Each one of them was fifteen feet tall. Ann's heart stopped as she realized what they were: dinosaurs!

The huge gorilla swung out his arm. *Crunch!* One of the dinosaurs crashed into a tree trunk. It released its grip on the ape's wrist with a whimper.

Blood ran in streams from the spot where the other dinosaur still clung to the ape's wrist. The ape reached over with his free hand, grabbed the dinosaur by the neck—and began to squeeze.

Ann had thought the giant gorilla was all she had to fear. But she was learning that this entire island was filled with monsters. Horrible creatures she couldn't even have imagined a few days ago.

Still choking the dinosaur, the ape dropped Ann. She hit the ground hard and lay there stunned. When she recovered, she quickly surveyed her surroundings. She moved only her eyes. She thought it was a good idea to pretend to be unconscious—at least for now. Maybe she could escape again while the two massive creatures battled. She heard them growling and grunting above her.

She lay in a decaying courtyard. Tall stone walls surrounded her on all sides, eroding into dust or being slowly pulled apart by the thick vines that grew all over everything in sight. No humans had used this place in hundreds of years. Beyond the crumbling walls, jungle lay thick in every direction.

The dinosaur thudded to the ground beside her, the impact shaking the ground like an earthquake. Ann gasped. The thing was dead. If she'd been a few feet to the left, she would be dead now, too. She would have been crushed beneath tons of dinosaur flesh.

The ape reached down and prodded her with one finger. Ann forced herself to keep her body limp. She didn't even resist when he rolled her over. Maybe he'd think she was dead and just leave her there. The beast growled. Ann felt his hot breath against her skin. It was hard to simply lie still, but she hoped he would lose interest in her if she didn't move.

It worked. The beast crouched over the dinosaur and began to feed. The ripping, slobbering sounds twisted Ann's stomach into a pretzel. It was easy to imagine the huge ape having her for supper.

She had no time to indulge her fears. This was her best chance to creep away. The ape was completely absorbed by the dead dinosaur. Ann looked around, trying to decide on the best escape route. A narrow stairway at one side of the courtyard looked like the best possibility. Maybe it would lead to a path.

She crawled toward it. Slowly, slowly, slowly. Any fast movement might catch the beast's attention. *Right hand, left leg, right leg, left hand,* she silently coached herself. *Slowly, slowly, slowly.*

Her gaze was locked on the staircase. She needed to get there before the giant gorilla finished with the dinosaur. A beast that big would have to eat for quite a while to satisfy his hunger. At least she prayed that was true. *Right hand, left leg, right leg, left hand. Slowly, slowly, slowly.*

Something ran over Ann's back. She twisted her neck and saw a bug the length of her arm skittering across the courtyard. Ann bit the inside of her cheek to keep from screaming. If she screamed, she would attract the attention of the ape. But she couldn't keep crawling, just waiting for the next giant insect to come along. She jumped to her feet. She'd made it about halfway to the staircase, and now she was ready to run.

Ann raced across the courtyard. Immediately she heard the ape let out a roar of protest. He had seen her. She didn't look back. She kept on running. She reached the narrow staircase and started to climb down.

The stairs ended in a grassy clearing. Bad news. It would be too easy for the ape to spot her in the vast open space. But there was no turning back. She tore across the field.

Wham!

The beast's massive fist slammed into the ground in front of her. The earth shook under Ann's feet and she toppled. She pushed herself upright and began her race to freedom again.

Wham!

The beast's fist went down. So did Ann. She felt like she was doing her slapstick act. Falling on her face again and again.

She didn't wait for the ape to lift his hand. She ducked underneath, feeling his coarse hair brush across her head. Her feet slid back and forth in the high grass.

Bam! This time she fell on her behind.

The ape squealed. He sounded almost like a happy five year old. An extremely large five year old. Ann used both hands to push herself upright—and immediately fell again.

The beast did everything but clap his hands. He was enjoying himself. *Keep on laughing, buddy,* Ann thought. *Just let me get away.*

She took three steps, and then landed on her back again. She tried to stand right away. But it was as if she was boneless. Exhaustion overcame her. She needed to rest. Just for a few seconds. Then she would try to flee again.

The giant ape gave a grunt. Ann didn't look up at him. Even turning her head was too much exertion. She was bruised and battered from being dropped by the ape, from the spills she'd taken on the ground, from bouncing around in the beast's massive hand, from being abducted from *The Venture*.

Ann's eyes began to burn with tears. It was all just too much. The ape flicked her with one finger. A jolt of pain shot through her. "Stop it, Kong!" she snapped. She figured since the villagers chanted the word *Kong* so often, it might be the beast's name. "I've had enough of you!"

Ann used every bit of willpower she possessed to climb to her feet again. She swayed. Her legs were unwilling to support her body. She crumpled.

Bam! Kong's fist hit the ground next to her. He wasn't a

happy five year old anymore. He was a cranky five year old whose favorite toy had broken. Ann stayed where she had fallen, trying to catch her breath, trying to find enough strength to stand once more. She didn't want to cry, but one tear escaped and rolled down her face.

Then, something amazing happened. The beast turned and walked away. Ann managed to sit up and stare after him. Kong looked over his shoulder at her. There was a message in his huge yellow eyes.

Go, his eyes said to her. *I won't follow you. You're free.*

8

The rescue party had entered the swamp. Filthy brown water stretched as far as the eye could see. Every so often a dead, twisted tree trunk rose from the surface of the fetid water. Thick gray fog drifted close over the muck. Nothing disturbed the view of this bizarre landscape, the only life in sight being the tiny lizards that seemed almost to fly from one tree trunk to the next. It was eerily silent.

Then a gentle splash filled the air.

"What was that?" Lumpy asked.

He looked back to a raft made of tree branches floating ten feet away. Jimmy, Choy, and a couple of sailors sat on the moving raft. Jack stood at the front, using a long bamboo pole to pull the raft through the swamp. A pack filled with ammunition was strapped to his back. He scanned the water, but didn't see anything moving in the mist.

Lumpy's raft floated in front of Jack's. Hayes steered that one, while Carl looked around and Lumpy continued to stare suspiciously into the water.

His imagination is running away with him, Jack thought. *Not that he blamed Lumpy after all that happened. He—*

Rancid water exploded into Jack's face as a huge creature leaped into the air, long and thin like an eel. But this wasn't an eel. When it opened its mouth, it looked more like a piranha. Jagged, daggerlike teeth filled the cavernous mouth.

There was no time for Jack or the others to flee or attack. The creature's teeth flashed as its powerful jaws smashed into Jack's raft, snapping the craft in half. Bits of wood and mud flew into the air. Jack tumbled into the water with a cry of surprise, the ammo pack still on his back.

"Jimmy!" Hayes called.

Jimmy splashed toward shore. Carl spotted Preston treading water, holding the camera up over his head to keep it from getting wet. *Jack? Where was Jack?* Carl wondered.

Hayes poled the other raft to the shore, his muscles straining as he moved the raft as fast as it would go. "Get them out of there! Help them!" Hayes yelled.

Lumpy reached out a hand to grab Choy, who splashed in the dark water five feet from the remaining raft. "Swim, you dopey bugger! Swim!" Lumpy shrieked.

But Choy sank beneath the surface.

Lumpy let out a growl of frustration, and then dove off the raft to save him.

Carl scanned the water for Jack. His eyes snagged on the camera—the camera and Preston. "Hold on, Preston!" he yelled. "Don't let go. Whatever happens, don't let go of the camera!"

Preston jerked sideways as a loud splash filled the air. He gasped as a huge serpentine body swam by, half in and half out of the water. Each of its scales was as big as a man's head.

Carl had to do something. He grabbed a tommy gun and managed to shoot in the direction of the creature. It disappeared from sight.

Preston turned about in the water. Jack's face appeared above the surface. He let out the breath he'd been holding.

"Swim, Preston," he growled.

With Jack's help, Preston managed to make it to shore. Carl stretched out a hand to pull his assistant onto dry land. Then he snatched the camera, cradling it as if it were a child he'd saved from certain death. Water ran from his wet hair down his face, forming tiny rivers through the mud that caked his skin. He fumbled with the camera, cranking it as fast as he could.

"Turn that bloody thing off," Lumpy ordered from his spot on the shore next to Choy, who was still coughing up water.

"Just a quick check," Carl argued, as his eyes roamed over the camera. A smile lit up his face. "It's working!"

Jack shook his head and gazed out over the swamp. There was no sign of whatever had attacked them. For a split second, everything was still. Then the head and shoulders of a sailor broke the surface. The man swam quickly toward land, pulling himself up out of the muddy water and wading onto shore. He grinned, relieved.

Jack grinned back. Then he saw a giant form rise silently behind the sailor. Up, up, up . . . the thing was at least twenty feet long, shaped like an eel or some sea monster from a child's nightmare. Its long, thin body arched over the sailor. It opened its mouth, its jaws impossibly wide. Its knifelike teeth were impossibly sharp. Jack opened his mouth to shout a warning—

Too late. The creature pounced, plunging down onto the sailor with lightning speed.

The jagged teeth flashed, digging into the sailor's body. The long, snakelike body rose again, dragging the poor man with it, up into the air, his legs kicking in agony.

Then the monster slid back down into the water, pulling the man under. The muddy surface barely showed a ripple where the sailor—and the monster—had been.

9

Ann had to find Jack and the others. They were here in the jungle somewhere, searching for her. If only she could reach them, she'd be safe and this terrible adventure would be over for good. But how could she even begin to look for them in this dense forest?

It was hot. Ann felt tired and thirsty. But the only water she could find was a tiny rivulet of dew running down the face of a humongous boulder covered in moss. She cupped her hands together and gathered as much as she could. She managed to get only one mouthful, but it eased her thirst enough for her to go on.

She made her way up a small hill. At the top there was a clearing, and Ann could see the sky for the first time since she'd left Kong. A plume of smoke rose in the distance, and she felt her heart sink. That smoke had to come from the village—or maybe from *The Venture*. Either way, it was too far for her to get to easily. The smoke had to be miles from where she stood.

Suddenly, Ann heard a sound in the forest behind her. Footsteps! She caught her breath. Could it be Jack? Had he found her at last?

Or was it something else?

The footsteps were closer now. Only a few feet away.

She couldn't risk it. She ducked behind a tree at the edge of the clearing—just as an eight-foot-tall dinosaur stepped from the jungle on the other side. Its scales were a mix of mottled browns and oranges, and it stood on two powerful legs that accounted for most of its body. Above those strong legs was a smallish torso with short arms that curled against its chest. Ann held perfectly still, unsure if it had seen her or not.

The dinosaur's nostrils twitched, and it raised its scaly head to smell the air. A rush of fear filled Ann's body. Could it *smell* her? What if dinosaurs could track a scent like dogs? This thing would find her and kill her for sure. As quietly as she could, she took a step backward. She turned around . . . and saw another mottled dinosaur! She was surrounded. There was no escape . . . except through the jungle.

As Ann thrashed her way through the branches and

vines, she heard the dinosaurs crashing after her. There was no way to outrun them. Their legs were as almost as tall as her entire body. Any second, they'd catch her.

Straight in front of Ann was a tall tree with roots that stretched out several feet in every direction around the trunk. The roots themselves were as thick as the trunks of mature trees back home—they would make a good hiding place. It was her only hope.

She sprinted for the tree and threw herself down between two huge roots. From there she could see that the tree was dead and its wood had begun to rot. One of the dinosaurs snapped at her, its terrifying teeth just inches from her face. Instinctively, Ann pulled away. The dirt underneath the roots gave way, and she sank farther into the hollow below the tree. She was safe for the moment.

But the dinosaurs weren't about to give up. They knew where Ann was, and they were determined to get at her. One of them began clawing at the roots above her, while the other rammed its snout into the opening. Hot, foul-smelling breath washed over Ann, and she gagged.

One of the dinosaurs let out a scream of anger, a piercing sound that sent shivers down her spine. She closed her eyes to shut out the sight of these monsters. Her heart was pounding so hard that she thought she might die of fear.

Then the nearest dinosaur flew into the air.

Ann stared up through the opening between the roots, baffled. These dinosaurs didn't have wings.

This one must have been lifted up. But by what?

She inched a bit closer to the opening . . . and spotted the dinosaur's legs. The legs flailed about in the air, flying from side to side. Then they gave a great spasm, and went limp. The dinosaur was dead.

The other one turned and fled into the jungle.

Ann wished she could follow it, because whatever had killed that dinosaur was big—big enough to pick up an eight-foot-tall beast and kill it. More important, whatever had killed that dinosaur was still out there, standing just feet away from her. And it would come after *her* next.

Keep still, she told herself. *Hold absolutely still and maybe it won't notice you.*

Just then, Ann felt pressure on her leg. She glanced down and saw a rope moving slowly across her thigh. A thick, black rope made of coarse hair. She gasped. That was no rope. It was a leg—a two-foot-long leg! Her throat went dry. Some other kind of monster was in here with her! Another leg crept out from underneath the tree and began moving across her body. Ann's breath came in shallow gasps as she tried to keep from screaming. She couldn't risk catching the attention of the thing outside.

But what was she trapped with in there?

Ann forced herself to study the creeping black legs. There was only one thing that could have legs like that. A giant spider. And judging from the length and thickness of its legs, this was the biggest one in history. The thing had to be almost as big as her.

She glanced up. Still no sign of whatever killed that dinosaur. Did Ann dare make a run for it?

A third leg crawled out onto her stomach. That did it. Whatever was out there, it couldn't be any worse than the giant spider that was in there with her. She crawled forward and hauled herself up between some roots on the other side.

The first thing she saw was a claw. One single deadly curved claw, at least a foot long, on a foot with two more matching claws. Ann's eyes traveled up the gigantic body to the impossibly big head, the smaller dinosaur still in its mouth.

She knew what it was. A Vastatosaurus rex, the most vicious dinosaur that ever lived.

Her body went stiff with fear. She staggered, forgetting to breathe as terror filled her. The V. rex fixed its small black eye on Ann as it chomped on its prey.

Some tiny voice in Ann's head was screaming for her to run as she stood there, rooted in place with fear. But she had no control over her limbs. The V. rex shook its huge head, sending bits of dead dinosaur flesh flying through the air. One piece splattered across her cheek. The warm wetness against her skin freed her from her paralysis. She fled.

The V. rex came after her. Each step it took brought it ten feet closer to her. There was no time to think—she acted on pure instinct. She spotted a fallen tree hanging out over the edge of a small cliff. It was strong enough to hold her, but it wouldn't support the weight of the monstrous dinosaur. She scooted out onto the moss-covered log. Below her, the drop was at least fifteen feet. Ann wrapped her arms around the tree and held on with all her strength.

The V. rex lifted its massive leg and stepped onto the log. The log gave a sickening lurch. The big dinosaur quickly retreated. It roared its anger, the sound almost deafening. Then it grabbed the end of the log in its claws—and dumped the entire thing over the side of the little cliff.

Ann fell through the air and landed with the heavy log on top of her. She winced, expecting its weight to crush her—but the limb skittered to the side, a section falling across her legs. She was still alive.

But she wouldn't be for long if she didn't get up. The fifteen-foot drop was nothing to the V. rex. It hopped down from the cliff as if it were stepping off a curb.

Ann backed away on her hands and tried to kick the rest of the log off her legs. But it was no good. The log was heavy, and she was exhausted and scared. She couldn't get up in time.

The V. rex lunged, its jaws opened wide to devour her. The last thing Ann saw was its razorlike teeth, dripping with saliva. Then she closed her eyes, waiting for death.

She could smell the dinosaur's foul breath. Suddenly she felt and heard nothing. There was a strange choking, whooshing sound.

Ann opened her eyes. It was Kong! He must've yanked the V. rex away from her at the last second. He sat astride the dinosaur, holding on to its neck as it twisted back and forth trying to bite him. Kong punched its head over and over with his mighty fists.

It was hard to believe, but Ann actually felt happy to see the monstrous ape. The V. rex's head hit the ground, and Kong reached out for her. She hardly even struggled as he lifted her in his massive hand.

Footsteps thundered through the jungle, and a second V. rex appeared through the trees, running full speed toward Ann and Kong. This one was slightly smaller—the mate of the dinosaur Kong had just fought. It clamped its jaws onto Kong's arm, and Ann thought she heard its teeth scrape against bone. The ape gave a mighty shake and threw the dinosaur free. But it came right back at him. Ann clung to one of Kong's fingers, turning her face away from the charging dinosaur . . .

. . . and toward another one! The first V. rex had gotten back to its feet. And another one was running from the jungle to join in the fight. This one looked different, younger. Was it their child?

Ann's head swam. Three huge, carnivorous dinosaurs attacking at once. How could any creature on earth survive such a fight? Even Kong, with his hideous strength, couldn't fight all three.

The ape whipped Ann away from the jaws of the first V. rex as it lunged for her. He tossed her through the air, catching her deftly in his other hand. She landed hard, the wind knocked out of her lungs. By the time she'd recovered enough to look around, Kong had jerked a tree from the ground with his other hand. He held it aloft, the massive

Ann Darrow was just an actress trying to make it in New York . . .

. . . until Carl Denham asked her to star in his next film. He had big plans for Ann.

SKULL ISLAND

Carl had discovered a map.
Skull Island would be the perfect
place to film his movie.

Jack Driscoll was hired to write the screenplay.
He works in the hold of The Venture, the ship
Carl chartered for his journey.

After arriving on Skull Island, the crew discovers the ruins and the people who live there.

The villagers have taken Ann and sacrificed her to a great beast. Only Carl saw what happened to her.

"What took her, Carl?"

Ann escapes Kong, but runs into more trouble.

6° 15'

92° 50'

93° 5'

92° 45'

Latitude 6° South from the Equator

6° 15'

92° 50'

93° 5'

Kong saves the day!

92°

East from Greenwich

Latitude 6° South from the Equator

Undeterred by Ann's disappearance, Carl keeps his cameras rolling.

Jack searches for Ann . . . and Kong.

South from the Equator

Kong becomes
Ann's protector.

Jack finally finds Ann and helps her escape.

The crew prepares to leave Skull Island . . . with Kong. What will happen to this giant gorilla in New York?

roots still dangling from the end. As the first V. rex charged again, Kong rammed the tree straight into its open mouth, pushing it out the back of the creature's neck.

Ann screamed in horror at the gruesome sight. The V. rex dropped to the ground, dead.

The second dinosaur reached for them. Kong fought hard, punching with all his strength, his actions matching his prizefighter face. But he was hampered by holding Ann—he could fight with only one hand at a time. Every so often, he shoved her back and forth between his giant fists. She was so battered and winded that she lost track of what was going on. All Ann could see was dark fur and huge teeth. She was too exhausted to be afraid.

A particularly loud snarl woke Ann from her daze, and she saw the face of the young V. rex only a few feet from her. It had leaped at Kong, going for his throat. The giant ape staggered backward, and suddenly his grip on her loosened. She tumbled from his hand and hit the ground—hard.

Stars exploded in front of Ann's eyes, but she forced herself to get to her feet and run. Kong had the second V. rex in a headlock and was trying to flip the dinosaur over his back. Both were too distracted by the fight to notice Ann. She ran as fast as her tired legs would go, heading for the cover of the huge trees nearby.

As she ran, Kong suddenly changed direction. In the middle of flipping the dinosaur, he reversed himself. The V. rex jerked back in the unexpected direction, and its spine broke with a sickening snap that echoed through the jungle. The V. rex went limp immediately.

Ann kept running. Suddenly, she swung up into the air. A sharp pain shot through her arm, and her entire body was bathed in moist, foul-smelling heat. She turned her head around to see what had happened.

The third V. rex had come up behind her as she ran. And now Ann was in its mouth.

Her vision blurred with tears. All around her was the heat and stench of the carnivore's mouth. One sharp tooth had grazed her arm, and she was pinned down by the pressure of it. As soon as the V. rex bit down again, Ann would be killed.

Her pulse thudded in her ears as she squirmed, trying to wrench herself from the dinosaur's mouth.

Kong's huge fingers appeared above Ann, and then below her. The pressure in her arm eased. She could move! Kong had grabbed the jaws of the V. rex and was pulling them open to free her.

The V. rex fell backward, struggling to loosen Kong's grasp. Ann began to slide farther into its mouth as it crashed to the ground. Frantically, she grabbed onto the only thing she could think of—a tooth. She held on until Kong had pulled the jaws wide enough for her to scramble out, her feet slipping and sliding on the dinosaur's tongue.

Breathing hard, Ann dragged herself from the mouth of the V. rex. Once she was free, Kong gave a mighty yank and pulled the dinosaur's jaws apart wider . . . and wider . . . until they broke. Its head split open along the jawline, and the V. rex was dead.

Ann sat in the grass, dazed, surrounded by death. Three humongous dinosaurs, dead. It was impossible to believe that Kong had done so much, that he could be so strong. She lifted her eyes to the giant ape.

He was beaten up. Blood oozed from the wound on his arm and from a dozen smaller cuts all over his body. Fur hung in tatters from a scratch on his cheek. But his eyes blazed with pride. He gathered himself up and let out a roar, his leathery hands beating his chest in a primal act of triumph.

As if to answer him, gunshots rang through the forest from somewhere nearby. Ann's heart leaped with hope . . . and fear. If Kong could kill three of the fiercest dinosaurs ever to walk the earth, what might he do to a group of mere men? Would guns ever be enough to slay this mighty ape?

Kong let out an even louder roar. He was ready to fight again.

His eyes fell on Ann, and he snatched her in his hand before she could move. He lifted her high into the air and carried her a little way into the jungle. All around them were the remains of some ancient temple. A tall, stone column stood, beginning to crumble but still proud, amid the ruins. It was thirty feet high, and Kong placed Ann on top of it. Then he stalked off into the forest, knocking aside trees as if they were mere twigs. He was going to kill her rescue party.

And Ann was trapped atop the column.

10

Jack, Carl, and the others had been searching for Ann for hours. Lumpy and Bruce were starting to grumble again, but Jack was sure Ann was still alive. She had to be—and they had to find her. He knew Hayes agreed with him. Hayes was a good man, and his service during the war had given him a strong belief that no one should be left behind. He'd keep looking for Ann until he found her, dead or alive. And the other sailors respected him. Jack hoped that would be enough to keep them all focused on getting to Ann.

It was tough going in the jungle—every plant, every tree, every rock was gigantic. The vegetation was so thick, Jack could only see five feet in front of him. He forced his way through a thorny bush and put his foot down . . . on nothing.

Jack jerked backward to regain his balance. He stood at the edge of a wide gash in the ground. It was a chasm so deep that the bottom was lost in darkness. Thick vines grew all across it, stretching from one side to the other and tangling together in giant webs. On the other side, crumbling stone slabs and columns peeked from the dense foliage.

A large tree had fallen across the chasm twenty yards away, creating a natural bridge.

Hayes stepped up onto the tree trunk. "Single file," he called. "Jimmy, you follow me. Don't look down."

Jimmy nodded, sticking close to Hayes. He climbed eagerly up onto the trunk—and immediately began to slip on the thick, slimy green moss that covered it. He stepped back off the tree trunk, took a deep breath, and then tried again.

Jack went next, Carl behind him. The rest of the party came after them in single file. The footing was treacherous—the moss was wet with dew, making it slippery. Jack inched across slowly, concentrating on keeping his balance.

Hayes was almost all the way across when he suddenly stopped. He stared straight ahead, studying the old stone ruins on the other side of the chasm.

"What is it?" Jimmy's voice sounded worried. "Mr. Hayes?"

"If anything happens, you run. Understand?" Hayes answered without turning around, his voice tight with tension. *What did he know?* Jack wondered, struggling to see into the jungle without falling off the log.

"I'm not a coward, I ain't gonna run," Jimmy told him.

"It's not about being brave, Jimmy," Hayes said, turning around. "I want you to make it back." His eyes locked on Jack's for a brief second, and Jack nodded. If anything happened, Jack would watch out for Jimmy. He wouldn't let the kid do anything stupid. If Hayes said to run, they'd run.

Hayes made his way to the other side and stepped down off the tree. In front of him, some of the ruins had collapsed on top of one another. They formed sort of a tunnel that the men would have to enter if they wanted to keep going. It was dark inside. Hayes walked slowly toward it, peering into the blackness.

Jimmy was almost to the end of the tree trunk. Jack followed his gaze through the tunnel.

Something looked back at him.

Couldn't be. Jack blinked. His imagination must be working on him. But no, the eyes were still there. Gleaming yellow in the darkness. And getting closer—fast.

"Go back!" Hayes shouted. He raised his tommy gun and fired into the tunnel.

Jimmy obeyed instantly. Jack spun around on the mossy tree, trying to run back to the other side. The other men tried, too. But everyone slipped and slid on the moss. Nobody managed to move fast enough. Jack shot a look over his shoulder. Hayes was sprinting for the log, still firing into the tunnel as he went.

The eyes came closer. Whatever it was, it was charging straight at them. And it didn't seem to mind the gunfire at all. The eyes turned into a face and a body as the thing burst out of the tunnel. It was a gorilla.

A monstrous gorilla. Twenty-five feet high, as wide as a building. The men cried out in shock when they saw it. All but Jack. He couldn't make his voice work.

That was the thing that took Ann. He knew it.

Hayes raced back up onto the tree trunk. The gorilla grabbed him, picking him up as if he were no bigger than a chipmunk.

"Shoot!" Jack yelled, raising his rifle.

His voice broke the shock that had paralyzed the rescue party. In one motion, the others lifted their guns and fired on the ape. Jack tried to aim away from Hayes in the thing's hand.

The gunfire was bothering the gorilla now. He roared and raised his fists in the air. Jack's stomach gave a lurch as the ape lifted his arm and hurled Hayes straight at them. He watched Hayes fly over his head, screaming the whole way. Then he crashed into the wall on the other side of the chasm. His neck tilted at an unnatural angle and he stopped screaming.

"Noooooooooo!" Jimmy cried. He charged at the gorilla.

Jack tackled him from behind, slamming himself and Jimmy down onto the log before Jimmy reached the end. Jack's face smashed into the moss just as the ape's huge fist smashed against the log just a foot away.

Jack rolled sideways as the fist slammed down again, almost hitting him and Jimmy. He grabbed onto one of the vines that stretched across the chasm, using it to keep his balance on the log. Jimmy reached for another vine snaking around the log and got a hold of it as the fist came down again.

Carl let out a yell as the log shook. He slid along on the moss, and his camera shot out of his arms. It fell, but not into the chasm. The thing got stuck in a little fork in the log. One more smash of the fist and it would shake free. Wild-eyed, Carl crawled along the tree trunk on all fours, trying to reach the camera. But Lumpy was closer.

"Grab it! Don't let it fall!" Carl yelled. That camera was Carl's life—if he managed to survive the island.

Lumpy's face twisted in a sneer. He lifted up his foot and kicked the camera loose. It tumbled down, down, down into the chasm.

Jack was glad to see it go. Carl's precious film was the reason they were on Skull Island. The reason Hayes and Herb were dead, and maybe Ann, too. It was the first time he'd actually allowed himself to think that about Ann. He shoved the thought out of his brain. She couldn't be dead. There still had to be time to save her.

The gorilla snarled. He reared up to his feet and grabbed the end of the tree trunk. He lifted it easily into the air and started to shake it. That was even worse than the pounding. The tree was so slippery that nobody could hang on. Jack clung to a vine, and so did Jimmy. But a few of the other sailors fell off into the chasm. Choy fell with them. His arms pinwheeled as he tried to grab onto anything that would save him. All he could reach was air. Lumpy screamed as his friend disappeared from sight.

The log swung violently—from side to side, up and down. The ape used all his strength to try to shake the men off. Preston was close to the end of the trunk opposite Jack and Jimmy. He leaped off, landing near the edge of the chasm. He grabbed onto a vine that grew over the edge, and pulled himself up to the top. But no one else was close enough to do that.

The gorilla roared again and lifted his end of the tree up over his massive head. He hurled it forward, into the chasm. The rescue party plummeted into the hole with it. Jack hung on tight to his vine and prayed that the tree wouldn't land on top of him.

It seemed to take forever for the tree to tumble to the ground. Vines smacked against Jack's face and body on the way. He saw Bruce fly off the log. He landed on a little shelf of rock, but Jack and the others kept falling.

They each landed with a thud. All the bones in Jack's body seemed to slam against one another, and the breath exploded out of his flattened lungs. For a moment, all was silent. Jack sat up and let go of the vine. His hands were scraped raw from clutching it, but it had saved his life. He blinked rapidly, trying to clear his vision enough to take in his surroundings: It was dark down here, and the ground was made of thick black mud.

Lumpy pushed past him, calling for Choy. Jack followed. Choy lay nearby in the mud, his body bent almost in half and his breathing shallow. He was dying. Lumpy knelt by his side.

"What do you think he say about this?" Choy asked.

"Who?" Lumpy asked, his voice thick with tears.

"My guy, Charlie Atlas," Choy said. "Training, see? Training make all the difference. Anyone else after a fall like that be curtains for sure."

Lumpy took Choy's hand. "I used to think it was a waste of time," he replied. "But you held up." His voice broke, and he let out a sob.

"Hey, don't worry. It's okay," Choy said. He was smiling. Then his eyes went blank, and Jack knew he was dead. Jack turned away. How many more men would they lose on this godforsaken island?

Jack's eyes fell on Hayes. His body lay ten feet from Choy's. Jimmy crouched over him, rocking back and forth in grief. Jack felt a ball form in his own throat. They'd all miss Hayes. But for Jimmy, it was like losing a father. Jack knelt next to the young sailor and put his arm around Jimmy's shoulders to comfort him, but Jack knew there was no comfort.

Lumpy cradled Choy's body in his lap while Jimmy cried over Hayes. Carl sat nearby, gazing at his shattered camera. A few tins of film lay nearby. Some of them were open. *Does it even matter?* he wondered for the first time, despair flooding through him.

Nobody spoke. Jack looked up to the top of the chasm. The gorilla was gone.

A strange sucking sound filled the air. The mud near Choy's body was moving. Jack let go of Jimmy and grabbed a long stick from the ground just as a gigantic, white thing wriggled up from the muck. It was a maggot—a six-foot-long maggot. He jabbed at it with the stick, trying to push the blind, seeking head of the thing away.

Lumpy grabbed Choy's body under the arms and tried to pull him away from the maggot. But more creatures appeared, the mud erupting as they squirmed up on all sides. They were huge, most of them the size of dogs. They were like visions from a nightmare—disgusting combinations, like a centipede mixed with a scorpion or a stickalithus crossed with a crab. All of them were giants, like everything else that lived on Skull Island.

They came up from the ground and from fissures in the rock walls of the chasm. One three-foot-long bug with curved, segmented pincers went after Choy's body. Lumpy hurled himself at it, trying to fight it off. But another bug grabbed him in its mandibles, and he fell. The bug was on him instantly, its massive jaws crunching on Lumpy's bones.

Jack heard him screaming, but couldn't watch as the bug ate Lumpy. He couldn't stand to see one more person die.

A stickalithus came at him—fast and silent. It was as huge as the pincer bugs, and it was vicious. Jimmy scrabbled around on the ground, searching for a stick of his own, as the stickalithus advanced. There were at least fifteen bugs behind it—clicking their pincers, writhing through the mud—and more arriving each second.

They were everywhere.

Carl went beserk. He grabbed a short stick and swung it like a club. He smashed a huge tapeworm as it bit his leg. White goo splattered his shirt, but he didn't stop swinging. He pulverized any bug that crossed his path. He was like a madman. It wouldn't help them, though, Jack realized. They were outnumbered and they were trapped.

Gunshots rang from up above. Instinctively, Jack dove for cover, pulling Jimmy down with him as bullets whizzed past their heads. The mutant bugs were blown apart, their innards splattering on the dank walls of the chasm. But how?

Jack got the answer as Bruce came down swinging on a vine like Tarzan, shooting as he went. More bugs appeared from holes in the dirt and stone as fast as he killed the others. Bruce couldn't stop them all.

Then more gunfire came from the top of the cliff. It was Captain Engelhorn! Other sailors from *The Venture* flanked him, all of them shooting the hideous bugs. They were saved!

Jack never thought he'd be so happy to see Bruce Baxter. When the actor landed in between him and Jimmy, Jack felt like hugging the man. "Nobody gets in my way," Bruce cried. "I'm an actor with a gun and I haven't been paid." He aimed at a huge earthworm and blew it away. The pieces of its segmented pink-and-gray body continued to squirm after it died.

A rope dropped from up above, and Preston yelled down, "Grab it!"

Jack pushed Jimmy toward the rope. "You first." He was going to make sure Jimmy made it back to the ship. He'd all but promised Hayes he would.

Jimmy grabbed onto the rope and climbed—fast. Preston and the others hauled the rope up as he climbed. Bullets flew past. The sailors were still shooting as more and more bugs appeared. It was as if the gunshots were making the things multiply. Preston threw the rope back down, and Bruce began to climb. Carl would go next. For now, he was still smashing things with his makeshift club, eyes bright with hatred.

The captain was clearly there to bring his men back to the ship. The rescue team had failed. But Jack couldn't give up. Ann was still out there somewhere, and he intended to find her. Even if he had to do it alone.

The rope dropped down in front of Carl. He was tempted to ignore it. Why should he go back up there? Why should he let himself be rescued and taken back to civilization? He slammed his club into a pincer bug's head until it was pulp, beating out his frustration. There was nothing there for him now. He was finished. He had no movie. He'd stolen film from the investors. He couldn't afford to pay Engelhorn. It was over. *He* was over.

But the survival instinct was strong. He grabbed onto the rope and began to climb. And the farther he rose into the air, away from those revolting bugs, the happier he felt. He'd get through this. He didn't know how, but he'd make it work. He'd salvage something from this ill-fated trip. He had no other choice.

When Carl got to the top, Engelhorn held out a hand to pull him up. "That's the thing about cockroaches," the captain said. "No matter how many times you flush them down the toilet, they always crawl back up the bowl."

Carl just laughed. "Hey, buddy, I'm outta the bowl. I'm drying off my wings and trekking across the lid!"

The captain shook his head. "The pity of it is you didn't die with the others."

Carl glanced at the faces of the sailors behind Engelhorn. They stared at him with venom in their eyes. They probably all agreed with their captain. It was his movie that had gotten them all into this mess. Preston couldn't even look him in the eye—he was that disgusted.

Sometimes that's the price you pay for greatness, Carl thought. *People don't understand you.*

He turned back to the chasm, waiting for Jack to appear at the top of the rope. But he wasn't there. He was on the other side—climbing up the vines to the top of the cliff across from Carl. Jimmy let out a whoop.

Carl shook his head, stunned. Jack was still going after Ann.

Leave it to his old friend Jack to write a twist ending to this sad story. He was gonna get Carl out of this mess—Jack was gonna save him.

"Driscoll, don't be a fool!" Engelhorn shouted furiously. "It's useless! Give it up. She's dead."

Carl stepped up beside him. "She's not dead," he said

quietly. "Jack's gonna bring her back. And the ape will be hard on his heels. We can still come out of this thing okay— if we put aside our differences. *More* than okay."

The captain looked Carl up and down, and gave a disdainful chuckle. "You want to trap the ape? I don't think so."

"Isn't that what you do? Live animal capture?" Carl pressed. "I heard you were the best."

Captain Engelhorn thought about it. Carl could tell he was intrigued by the idea—and that's all it took. Carl knew he had the man hooked.

"Look after yourself!" Carl called to Jack.

Jack waved. "Keep the gate open!" Then he took off into the jungle, running after Ann.

Kong carried Ann in his hand, but his fist wasn't tight anymore. He held her gently, almost cradling her. She clung onto one giant finger to keep herself from being jostled. She could hardly believe it herself, but she almost felt safe now. She was still scared, but it was nothing compared to the fear she'd felt when the vastatosaurs were attacking them. Kong had rescued Ann from them, and it was almost impossible for her to believe that he'd gone to so much trouble—and gotten so beat up—just because he wanted to kill her himself.

Ann wondered where he'd gone when he left her on top of that column . . . and what he'd done. All she knew was that he'd vanished into the jungle. Then she'd heard roaring and gunfire. When he came back, Ann could see he'd been shot in a few places. The wounds were small and didn't seem to bother him.

But what had happened to the men who'd shot him? Were they all right? Was Jack with them? Ann didn't think she'd ever find out. They couldn't keep coming after her at the expense of their own lives. Sooner or later, they'd give up and leave the island.

Kong was moving quickly through the jungle, heading toward an inconceivably tall hill. Ann wondered if it was the base of a mountain—the top was lost in fog. They came to a low chasm, ten feet wide. Without hesitation, Kong leaped across, reaching out for a thick vine on the other side.

The vine came loose in his giant hand, pulling an entire network of vines and branches down with it. Kong fell backward, holding Ann against him to protect her from the fall. She landed on his chest as he hit the ground with a thud. Before she could move, the mighty ape scrambled back to his feet, growling. He put Ann on the ground and pushed her behind him, as if to protect her from something.

Was it another dinosaur? Some other monster?

Ann peered around Kong's huge body. A face looked back at her from behind the vines. It was a carving, looming out from the wall of the chasm. It had been hidden by the vines until Kong pulled them down.

Kong snarled, challenging the face. He dropped into a

fighting stance, immediately on the defensive. Ann caught her breath, suddenly understanding. Kong thought the face was real.

"It's all right," she told him. "It's okay." Ann knew he couldn't understand her. But she wanted to help him. For the first time, she realized how hard the huge ape's life must be. Even though he was big and powerful, every day, every moment was a battle for survival. When he was faced with something unknown to him, his first instinct was to fight.

Ann thought of her life back home, constantly searching for the next acting job, the next paycheck. She knew how it felt to fight for survival.

She hurried over to the wall and pulled away the vines and the creepers to reveal the entire carving—a life-size, lifelike eroded statue of a sitting gorilla. A giant gorilla. It was the image of Kong.

"Look, it's you," Ann told him. "Kong. See? You. Kong. This is you."

Kong stared at the stone gorilla. Then he looked down at his own huge, leathery hands. Fear and sadness filled his eyes. Slowly, he picked Ann back up and turned away, subdued. He headed for the base of what Ann was now sure was a mountain.

Kong began climbing. He climbed for what seemed like an hour. Ann knew he would never drop her, but still couldn't make herself look down.

A bat flew past them, humongous like all the other animals on Skull Island. It screeched when it saw Ann, and swooped close. Its feet had sharp, hooked talons that stretched toward her. Up close, the creature was hideous—grayish-blue skin stretched tightly over a thin, bony body. Its face looked more like a lizard than a bat. One huge, curved fang protruded from the center of its mouth. Its eyes were cold, seeing Ann only as prey.

Kong curled his arm, pulling Ann in close against his body to protect her from the bat. With an angry cry, the bat swung away and flew off.

Finally, they reached the top of the mountain. They had to be a thousand feet in the air, with the jungle below them on all sides. A cliff jutted out over the vast forest, with a large round cave in the rock wall that rose behind it. Ann could tell this was where Kong lived as soon as she saw the cave. It was the only place large enough to hold him.

Kong placed Ann down near the entrance to the cave and loped over to the edge of the cliff. The sun was setting, turning the sky a brilliant orange color. The mighty ape sat huddled at the edge of the cliff, not looking at her.

She stepped into the cool darkness of the cave. Inside lay a skeleton, gleaming pale white in the darkness. A mighty rib cage, a massive skull. Tears sprang to Ann's eyes. These were the remains of a mighty gorilla, maybe Kong's mother or father. Judging by the statue in the jungle and this skeleton, it seemed that Skull Island had once been home to several such giants. But Kong was alone here. Was he the last of his kind?

Ann turned back to watch him as he sat silhouetted against the fiery sky. He was lonely and sad. She could feel it. How many times had she sat in her tiny apartment feeling just as alone, wishing for a family of her own?

Something moved deep within the stone cave. She heard a screech. No, many screeches, and the whisper of leathery wings rubbing together.

The bats, Ann realized. This cave is where they lived, too. Did Kong have to fight other creatures even in his own home?

Frightened, she hurried out of the dark cave and over to Kong. If any of the bats came for her, he would stop them. She knew it. He would protect her.

"Kong?" Ann murmured.

The big ape turned away from her.

Ann did a little tap dance, trying to amuse him. He'd liked her pratfalls, after all. But Kong still didn't look at her.

She wasn't willing to give up. She grabbed a stone from the ground and rolled it up and down her arm—a trick that the vaudeville audiences loved when she performed it with a top hat. But Kong didn't react.

"Look at me," Ann begged him. She tugged on one of his huge fingers. "Look at me."

Finally, he did. His eyes were filled with misery. Ann's heart went out to him.

She gazed out over the island. Far off in the distance, she saw *The Venture* anchored in the sea. So they hadn't left yet. But it was only a matter of time. Ann didn't want to watch, didn't want to know when they abandoned her. So she raised her eyes and looked at the horizon. The ocean stretched as far as she could see, with the last evening rays lighting a path across the water and straight up to the island. A large rain cloud moved across the sky in the distance, casting a shadow on the rippling golden water.

"It's beautiful," Ann said.

Kong growled softly, almost as if he understood her.

She looked into his eyes. "Beautiful," she repeated. She

put her hand on her heart, trying to make him feel what she felt. *"Beau-ti-ful."*

He stared at Ann for a moment, then opened one of his big hands. It was an invitation, she knew. And she wasn't afraid of him, not anymore.

Ann climbed into his palm.

He lifted her up and looked at her. Then, gently, he touched her hair with one huge finger.

Once Jack left Carl and Engelhorn behind, he moved fast. The ape's trail—*Ann's* trail, he hoped—was easy to follow. The path led straight to a mountain, and then it disappeared. That could only mean one thing: The ape had climbed up.

Jack began to climb.

It wasn't easy. There were stretches of rock with no footholds, and Jack didn't have a rope. But the thought of Ann in the grip of that monster kept him going. He had to save her. Enough people had died on this island. Ann Darrow wasn't going to die, too.

By the time Jack reached the top, it was dark. Luckily, the moon was almost full, and it cast a silver light over the jungle below him. He pulled himself over the lip of the last cliff and sat for a second trying to catch his breath. But he couldn't rest for long. He had to get to Ann!

He followed the ledge around a curve. A sheer rock face rose up from one side. Jack squinted into the darkness, making out the entrance to a cave in the stone wall. And in front of the cave lay the ape. His giant hairy back was to Jack, but Jack could tell by the way the beast was breathing that he was asleep.

Something moved inside the cave, stirring the air. Did anything live in there? Another gigantic ape? Some other huge creature? Jack had no time to check. He moved toward the gorilla, trying to be silent. He didn't want to wake it up—he just wanted to find Ann.

Where was she? Jack didn't see her in the cave. He circled the big ape until he could see its face. Its arms lay curled in front of its chest, and in one of its hands Jack saw her. Ann, sleeping peacefully in the grasp of the monster.

Finally he'd found her! She was less than ten feet away. But how could he reach her when the ape held her in his hand?

There was another noise from the cave. The gorilla growled in his sleep, and Jack drew back. The noise woke Ann. She opened her eyes and looked right at him. Her face lit up in happiness and surprise, and she opened her mouth to speak.

No! Jack thought. They couldn't risk waking the ape. He quickly put a finger to his lips to tell her to be quiet, and she nodded. She began moving slowly out of the giant hand. Jack stepped toward her.

The noise came from the cave again, louder this time. Suddenly, an immense bat appeared from the darkness at the back of the cave. It ran forward on taloned feet, and then spread its wings and flew from the cave. Its wingspan must have been at least eight feet wide.

Ann rushed toward Jack. He reached for her hand. Their fingers touched—and the giant gorilla's eyes snapped open.

Fear shot through him. He had to get Ann out of there *now*. He tried to grab her wrists so he could yank her away from the ape. But the creature was too fast for Jack. The ape's thick fingers closed around Ann with lighting speed. Jack saw her gasp for breath as the gorilla rolled away from him and got to his feet. Kong loomed over Jack, the gorilla's scarred face forming a terrifying snarl.

Behind him, Jack saw a giant bat swirl through the air. Then another. But he couldn't worry about them right now. He had to fight the ape. And he didn't even have a gun anymore.

"Jack, run!" Ann yelled. She was struggling in the

hand of the beast, but he wasn't about to let her go. Kong swatted at Jack with his other hand, ignoring Ann's cries of protest.

Jack jumped out of the way, but there was nowhere else to go. He was trapped between the edge of the cliff and the cave. Bats poured from the cave—and the drop from the cliff was probably a thousand feet. There was no escape. The ape would keep attacking him, and eventually the ape would win.

The massive ape swung at Jack again. "No!" Ann screamed. She pounded on the ape's hand with her fists. Jack doubted the beast could even feel it.

Kong reached up and put Ann down on a small ledge over the mouth of the cave. Now he had both hands free to hit Jack. Jack took a deep breath. The ape charged. Jack ducked and jumped around behind the ape. Kong whirled and growled at Jack, getting madder every second. He raised his muscled arm and smashed his fist down. Jack jumped to the side. *Wham!* Kong's other fist came down. Jack fell to the other side. Kong stamped his foot, missing Jack by less than a yard. Jack was out of breath already. He couldn't take much more. He stumbled and landed on his knees.

The ape raised his arm for one last blow.

Kong raised his fist to kill Jack. "No, please!" Ann
screamed. But of course Kong didn't understand her.
He continued to attack, and Jack had nowhere to run. If he
died, it would be Ann's fault—Jack was up on this ledge
only because he'd come to save her. Tears filled her eyes as
she saw Kong's arm start the fatal swing.

A screech rang through the air. One of the huge bats rose
in front of Ann, its dark, hairless wings filling the sky and
blocking her view of Kong and Jack. It dove straight for Ann.

She dropped to the ground, screaming. She covered her
head with her hands and screamed again as the bat raked her
with its sharp claws. Blood trickled down her arm.

Kong let out a roar and rushed at Ann, snatching her up
in his hand before the bat could strike again. As he lifted
Ann into the air, she looked frantically around for Jack. He
was there, pressed against the rock near the mouth of the

cave, staring up at Kong. Relief rushed through her. Jack was still alive!

She had only a moment of exhilaration, though, because the bat swooped in for another attack. And it had help. More bats poured out of the cave and swarmed around them. Each one was gigantic, and each one was vicious. They flew at Kong in groups, diving at him like a battalion of fighter planes.

Kong bellowed in pain. He held Ann close against his chest, trying to keep the bats away from her. They were fiercely tearing into him, their vicious talons ripping through his thick fur, and he couldn't fight them off with only one hand. Still roaring, Kong bent and put Ann down against the rock wall in front of the cave mouth. He began swatting at the bats with both arms, knocking them to the ground. They lay there stunned, red eyes staring blankly. Even more bats kept coming, diving at his face and body.

Ann turned to look for Jack. He was only a foot away, pressed against the wall. His eyes met hers, and he gave her a reassuring smile. He reached for her hand and pulled her toward him. There was no way out of there except to go past Kong and climb all the way back down the mountain. How could they escape?

Jack led Ann to the edge of the cliff, far above the jungle.

He grabbed onto a vine that grew over the ledge. Her stomach clenched as she realized what he expected her to do. She had no idea if his plan would work, but what choice did they have? She held onto his shoulders and closed her eyes as he lowered them both over the cliff.

Ann heard Kong bellowing above, and the bats screeching as they continued to attack him. She and Jack were getting farther and farther away—they swung on the vine at least sixty feet below Kong's lair.

Up above, there was a sudden silence. Had Kong beaten all the bats? Or had they somehow managed to kill the giant ape?

The answer came a moment later. Kong let out an enraged roar. Then the vine began to rise. He was pulling them back up!

Jack moved faster, trying to get them lower, but Kong was too strong. They were helpless as the gorilla tugged them up to him. At the top of the cliff, bats were still circling. They began to dive at Jack and Ann.

Ann looked up. Kong was staring over the cliff, eyes locked on her as he yanked up the vine.

A bat flew at Jack, and a plan slammed into his brain. He had no idea whether or not it would work, but he had to risk it. He took one hand off the vine and grabbed for the flying monster, catching hold of its ankle. "Hang on to me!" he called to Ann.

Ann tightened her hold on his shoulders as he took his other hand off the vine. He reached out and caught the bat's other ankle. The creature screamed angrily and flapped its giant wings, but Jack held on tight.

Dragged down by their weight, the bat plummeted toward the jungle floor as Kong roared his fury up above.

Ann's grip on Jack started to slip as they flew lower. The bat wobbled in the air, exhausted from the effort of trying to fly with them holding on. She glanced down. A river rushed along below them. Suddenly Jack let go of the bat.

Ann screamed as they fell through the air and plunged into the water. It closed over her head, and she felt a strong current sucking at her. She couldn't see Jack. She forced her way to the surface and managed to gulp in some air before the current jerked her over a waterfall.

Her stomach lurched as she felt herself falling again. But the waterfall was small, and the river below it moved more slowly. Finally, she could catch her breath. She treaded water and looked around for Jack. There he was—swimming for the bank. Ann followed him, dragging herself up onto the muddy shore. They both collapsed, too tired to move any farther.

"Jack?" Ann said. "Did he follow us?"

Jack sighed. "I think it's safe to assume he will." His plan with the bat had worked. But they weren't even close to safety. Not yet.

Ann thought about that. He was right. Kong would follow. He would come to save her—at least that's how he would think of it. He would try to save her from Jack the same way he saved her from the dinosaurs and the bats. The ape could never understand that Jack was trying to save her, too.

"Thank you," Ann said to Jack.

"For what?"

She smiled. "For coming back."

13

This would be Carl Denham's greatest triumph yet! Capturing the ape—it was a stroke of genius! If Carl couldn't bring Skull Island to the world through his film, at least he'd bring a little piece of it back alive. Well, a *big* piece of it.

He and the others were set up just inside the wall of the village. Outside, there was a chasm between the wall and the jungle—to keep the beast away. The entire wall on that side was lined with sharpened bamboo spikes. The only way across was over the altar bridge—a contraption, made of logs lashed together with vines, that looked like a huge crane. It could be slowly raised and lowered by pulling on a rope inside the wall. But if you simply cut the vine rope with a machete, the thing would slam down . . . fast.

Carl made sure the bridge was up. There was no way to get across the chasm to the gate. It was the only way his plan would work: Jack and Ann would be the bait for the trap. They'd come running for the gate, the mighty ape on their trail. If he allowed them into the village with time to spare, the beast would see that they were out of his reach. He might give up, go back to his lair.

So Carl's plan was to trap Jack and Ann on the other side of the chasm until the ape was right on top of them. Then he'd order the sailor already in position beside the rope to let the bridge down—when the beast was close enough to capture. Preston kept giving Carl the stink eye. He clearly thought Carl was putting his friends in danger. But Carl knew nothing could go wrong. He knew Ann and Jack would forgive him once his live "King Kong" show made them all rich.

Soon enough, Carl heard it—the ape, roaring and smashing through the trees. When Jack and Ann arrived outside the walls, the beast was close behind them. Carl and the others could all hear its vicious snarls. And they were screaming—Carl's friends Ann and Jack—screaming for their lives, begging them to lower the bridge. Carl knew they thought everyone had abandoned them, just hauled anchor and left them in this godforsaken place. It tore him up, but he had to wait until the ape was closer to the gate. He'd apologize to Jack and Ann later.

"Drop the bridge!" Jack called. "Carl!"

"Help us! Please!" Ann screamed. "Anyone!"

The roaring of the ape grew louder. Closer. Carl exchanged a glance with Engelhorn. Just a few more seconds . . .

"Drop the bridge!" Preston snapped. "Do it *now.*"

"Not yet," Carl told him. "Wait."

"No, Carl." Preston's mouth was set in a grim line. "You don't make the rules, not anymore."

He stalked over to the sailor manning the rope that controlled the bridge. Preston grabbed the machete from the sailor and swung it at the rope in one quick move. The vine rope snapped, sending one end flying into the air. It slashed Preston's cheek and he began to bleed.

Outside the wall, the bridge slammed down.

It was time to spring the trap.

There was a deafening boom. Jack grabbed Ann's hand, and they sprinted across the bridge, running as fast as they could toward the huge wooden gate. Kong was only a few feet behind them. They had to get into the village before he grabbed them! A hole had been blown in the gate near the bottom. Ann climbed through it and stopped, confused.

Carl just stood there inside the village, staring at Kong and the gate Kong was pounding on. Carl had such a strange look in his eyes—obsession, almost madness. He didn't even glance at Ann or Jack. No hugs, no sighs of relief, nothing.

And then Ann noticed the sailors. There were groups of them all over the village, hiding behind rocks and buildings. And they all had grappling hooks. She looked again at Carl, who stood near the gate. She noticed Preston, holding a rag to a bleeding cut on his face. And Captain Engelhorn holding a dark bottle.

"What are you doing?" Ann asked.

The captain barely looked at her. "Get ready."

Then there was an uproar at the gate. Kong had been pounding on it the whole time, and the bamboo was no match for his mighty fists. With a loud splintering sound, the wooden poles gave way, falling apart like a pile of pickup sticks. Kong had smashed through the gate.

"Bring him down!" Carl yelled to the captain. "Do it!"

Kong's eyes met Ann's, and he reached out for her. That's when she understood. They wanted to capture him.

"Now!" yelled the captain. All the sailors threw their grappling hooks, using the attached ropes to try to pull Kong down.

"No!" Ann cried, turning to Jack.

"Are you out of your mind, Carl?" Jack demanded. Anger at Carl's betrayal boiled through him. He had risked Ann's life—both their lives—to capture the ape.

Carl didn't answer.

Sailors had appeared on top of the wall. "Drop the net!" Captain Engelhorn called to them. The sailors had a giant net from the ship, weighted down on all sides by big boulders sewn into the netting. At the captain's order, they threw the boulders. The net sailed over Kong's head, and he fell to the ground. He thrashed around under the net, but the boulders held it in place over him.

"Gas him," Carl said.

That must be what was in the dark bottle the captain held, Jack realized—chloroform. But there wasn't a cage in the hold big enough to hold Kong. What was the man thinking? The giant ape was no rhino or lion or ordinary jungle animal that could easily be brought down and hauled off by Engelhorn's crew.

Kong's eyes were still on Ann. She could see the fear in them. Kong didn't understand what was happening. Ann began to cry. Kong didn't deserve to be treated this way. He wasn't evil—he was just wild. And he had protected her.

"No," she begged the men. "Please don't do this." She tried to run to Kong, but Jack held her back.

"Ann, he'll kill you," he said.

But Ann knew the truth. Kong wouldn't hurt her, not ever. "No, he won't," she insisted.

Nobody listened to her. The captain threw the bottle of chloroform, smashing it on the ground right under Kong's face. The giant ape breathed in the gas as he tried to push himself up against the weight of the net holding him. "Keep him down!" the captain yelled. The sailors on the wall lobbed rocks at Kong, pummeling his head. Ann could almost feel the blows on her own flesh. The captain pulled another bottle of chloroform from a nearby case and prepared to throw it.

"Stop it!" Ann yelled. "You're killing him."

"Get her out of here! Get her out of his sight," Captain Engelhorn told Jack.

Jack grabbed her arm. The captain was right. The sight of Ann seemed to be maddening the creature.

Kong roared, angry now instead of frightened. Ann knew what he was thinking—he thought Jack was attacking her. "Let go of me," she said quickly.

But it was too late. Kong exploded with rage. He rose to

his feet, tearing the net to pieces with his strong arms. He pulled at the ropes attached to him by grappling hooks, yanking sailors through the air. They couldn't keep him captive. He was too strong.

"Kill it!" the captain yelled.

"No!" Carl cried. This time, Ann agreed with him.

"It's over, you lunatic!" Captain Engelhorn said. "Shoot it!"

To Ann's horror, Jimmy grabbed a gun and started shooting at Kong. But the ape didn't seem hurt—it only made him angrier. He picked up a sailor and hurled him through the air. He charged at Jimmy, pushing an entire stone hut over in his rage.

The captain shoved Jimmy toward the path that led back to the dark tunnel and the stairs to the beach. Everyone else was running, too. Jack pulled Ann by the arm. He had to get her to safety. They had to escape Kong's rampage.

"Get to the boat!" Captain Engelhorn screamed. "All of you! Run!"

Jack took the steep stairs two at a time, dragging Ann behind him. All his energy was focused on getting to the beach.

Several lifeboats were lined up on the sand. He pulled Ann toward the nearest one. After everything he'd gone through to save her from the gorilla, he wasn't about to let the monster get her now. He didn't want the animal killed. But it was them against the Kong, their lives or his.

Ann fought to break free from Jack's grip. She couldn't let them kill Kong. But Jack was too strong. He wouldn't release her.

Jack skidded to a stop in front of the closest boat. Ann refused to get in. She turned back to watch the ape. "It's me he wants. I can stop this," she said.

Over my dead body, Jack thought. He wasn't giving her back to that monster. It would be condemning her to live on this island forever.

Kong smashed his way down the path from the village. Jimmy was shooting at him again, even though the bullets made no difference. He wanted revenge on Kong for killing Hayes. Jack understood that. But the kid was going to get himself killed. He had to do something. He couldn't let go of Ann, though. She'd run straight to Kong. Jack looked around. The only one nearby was Bruce. He'd have to do. "Take her!" Jack told him and shoved Ann into Bruce's arms. Bruce pulled her into the lifeboat.

"Let me go to him," she pleaded.

Jack turned away from her. He couldn't let her go to

Kong. The captain was yelling at the sailors to row the lifeboats out to sea. Jack ran across the sand to Jimmy and yanked the young sailor toward him, forcing Jimmy into the second lifeboat. Jimmy was still trying to shoot the ape as they attempted to escape.

Kong was on the beach now, charging straight for the boats. For Ann. She signaled for him to go back, even though she knew it was hopeless.

A few sailors pushed Jack's boat into the water. Carl splashed after them. He climbed into the boat and started rooting around on the floor. He came up with another bottle of chloroform. There was a whole crate full down there. Jack couldn't believe it—Carl was still trying to capture Kong. He held up the bottle to hurl it at the ape.

Just then, Jimmy fired another burst of bullets at Kong. The gorilla roared in fury and sped into the water after them. He raised his immense fist and smashed it down on the bow of the boat. The small boat rocked wildly from side to side, taking on water. Carl was flung overboard, still clutching his precious bottle of chloroform.

Kong grabbed the bow in his hands and swung, slamming the boat against the stone wall of the cove. The lifeboat splintered, smashed to bits. Jack and the others fell into the ocean. He tried to keep a hold on Jimmy as they were submerged. He was afraid the kid would do something stupid if Jack let him go.

When Jack got his head above water, Jimmy was next to him, coughing. Jack turned to look at Kong, but he wasn't paying attention to them anymore. He was watching Ann's boat. Bruce and Engelhorn were in the boat with her, scrambling around for weapons. Ann stared back at the big gorilla. She called to Kong. "Go back!"

Jack swore the ape understood her. Kong paused, as if sensing her fear for him.

Engelhorn found what he was looking for. He stood up in the boat, a harpoon gun in his hands. "Hold her," he said. Bruce grabbed Ann to keep her from getting in the way as Captain Engelhorn fired a harpoon into Kong's knee. The gorilla screamed in pain. Ann screamed along with him as the creature sank down into the water.

Ann sobbed as the captain loaded another harpoon, getting ready to kill Kong.

"Wait!" Carl yelled. Somehow he'd managed to pull himself up onto a rock in the water. He still had that bottle of chloroform. Carl had one last chance to make a life for himself back home, and he was going to take it. Capturing the beast would bring in enough money to keep him out of prison and make him the talk of the town.

Engelhorn paid no attention. He got ready to shoot the ape.

Kong was still staring at Ann. Even with a spear in his knee and a hundred bullet wounds, he began crawling after her.

"Leave him alone!" Ann yelled at the captain. She fought against Bruce, who held her tight. All she wanted was to reach Kong. He was in so much pain. He needed her.

Jack felt helpless there in the water. Jimmy was unconscious now—he'd sucked down too much seawater. Jack couldn't let him go. He couldn't help Ann . . . or Kong.

Just as the captain readied his shot, Carl hurled the chloroform bottle at Kong. It smashed against his cheek, releasing its gas. Kong choked. In his last seconds of consciousness, the beast reached for Ann, and she could feel her heart shattering.

Then the chloroform got him, and he slumped into the water, finally unconscious.

Jack met Ann's gaze. She was crying. She thought they were all barbarians.

And he couldn't blame her.

Carl wished he had his camera for that final moment on

Skull Island: the monstrous ape finally brought down, half in the water and half out. What a shot it would have been! What an end to his picture!

It didn't matter. He could visualize the new show now—not a film, but a live-action extravaganza: Kong, the Eighth Wonder of the World. He'd get Jack to write the story. Ann could star in the re-creation, he promised himself, trying to ignore the sound of her inconsolable sobs as she stared at the motionless beast. They'd all be millionaires.

The whole world will pay to see this. Carl Denham's name would go down in history: The Man Who Brought King Kong to New York!

EPILOGUE

Crowds thronged to the theater on opening night to see Carl Denham's new show: The Eighth Wonder of the World. No one knew exactly what to expect. They only knew the famous filmmaker and adventurer had come back from an unknown island, bearing an exotic prize. For a metropolis in the grip of the Great Depression, any excuse for entertainment and mystery was enough. The whole city wanted to see what Carl Denham had captured halfway around the world.

The box office on that fateful night was smashed to smithereens, so nobody will ever know for sure how many people were there. The police reports estimate that at least two thousand souls were packed into their seats when Denham unveiled the mighty beast-god Kong.

Two thousand people watched in awe as the gorilla was offered a fake sacrifice, a woman who was not his beloved

Ann Darrow. Two thousand people screamed in horror when the beast broke free from the chains that bound him to a three-story-tall scaffolding. Two thousand people were trapped in the theater while the giant ape rampaged among them, leaving death and destruction in his wake.

No one has ever known how Kong found Ann Darrow that night. Manhattan was in chaos. The ape stalked the streets with no regard for human life. Cars were overturned, buildings smashed, pedestrians crushed under his immense feet. Jack Driscoll would give no interviews afterward, but Carl Denham's assistant guessed that the ape had spotted Driscoll in the theater and followed him to Ann Darrow.

But the incredible truth is that *Ann* found *Kong*. Ann Darrow heard the sirens from ten blocks away; she heard the beast roaring, and she guessed what had happened. She knew all about Carl's show, but she wanted no part of it. She had stayed away. Now she suspected the worst. She could just imagine Kong stomping through the city in fury. She knew Kong would continue to attack without mercy, just like on the beach at Skull Island. And she knew only one thing could stop him: her. So she sought him out and found him, and he took her into the night.

But she could not save him as he had saved her so many

times. Even though she could tame the wild beast, she could not tame the violence in the hearts of men. The police and the army pursued Kong even when he stopped his vicious attack on the city. They pursued him to the top of the tallest building. They pursued him to his death.

Ann understood that what drove the ape was a desire to protect her, and so she grieved for Kong for the rest of her life. His need to protect her had been his undoing. If only he had stayed on his high mountain, Kong would have lived out his life in the jungle where he belonged. Instead, he had followed Ann to the village, to the beach . . . and to New York and his own death. Her beauty drew him in. And beauty killed the beast.